A ROSETTE for HELEN

A ROSETTE *for* HELEN

Doreen Bairstow

Scripture Union
130 City Road, London EC1V 2NJ.

© Doreen Bairstow 1991
First published 1991
Reprinted 1994

ISBN 0 86201 716 5

Phototypeset by Input Typesetting Ltd, London
Printed and bound in Great Britain by Cox & Wyman
Ltd, Reading

To Jasmine

Chapter One

'Oh, Mum, please say I can go – honestly, if you let me go on this holiday I won't ask for anything ever again – PLEASE say yes – I'll save up and help pay for it – please – I want it more than anything else in the world . . .'

Mrs Carter smiled and looked up from the dinner she was preparing. She couldn't help thinking how much her daughter, Jo, reminded her of how she had been at her age. Jo had just had her thirteenth birthday and was full of enthusiasm – for some things – and madly in love with ponies and riding – and anything to do with stables! The stables were offering a special 'Own a Pony for a Week' holiday and Jo and her friend, Clare, and all the other girls who spent every Saturday helping at their local riding school were desperately trying to get a place. 'I'll even wash up every day – without grumbling,' Jo added, to give extra weight to her plea. 'And Clare's going – in fact, I think half our class could go if they asked their parents – *please*, Mum.'

'Listen, Jo,' said Mrs Carter, drying her hands on the hand towel, 'whether the whole *school* is going makes no difference. Your dad and I will have to talk about it and decide. Now, please, love, just clear a space on this table. I'm trying to cook our dinner.'

Jo picked up her homework and made for the door. 'You won't forget, will you?' she called back over her shoulder.

Mrs Carter grinned.

'Forget what, dear?'

'Oh, Mum! It's not funny! I'm really serious. Please will you and Dad say I can go?'

'I told you, Jo – we'll talk about it.'

'How did you get on?' Clare asked Jo the next morning. But she could tell by the look on Jo's face. 'They said I can go!' The words almost came out in a squeal, and both friends gave each other a quick hug. They could hardly wait for break time at school to talk properly about it. It was hard concentrating on French and Geography when your mind was on other things. 'I hope I get Nelson to ride,' said Clare.

'Oh, and I want Barney,' crooned Jo. 'Imagine owning him for a week! He's brill! You can get the best shine ever on a coat like his – and I jumped him last week. He was great!'

'Are you going on the "Own a Pony Week"?' said a voice behind them. Jo and Clare turned to see Helen, a new girl who had recently come into their class. Helen was a shy, pretty girl with dark brown curls, and quite a bit smaller than Jo, who was tall and long-legged. Helen was finding it hard being in a new town and a new school. She missed her old friends and longed to make some new ones.

'What if we are?' said Jo, sharply.

'Oh, it's just that I go riding, too, and I've booked to go on the holiday. I wondered if I could come with you – I don't really know many people,' Helen added a bit lamely.

8

'Well, you could,' said Clare, not really liking her butting in on their friendship, 'but we're not in the beginners' group. We've both been riding about two years – and can trot and canter and jump a bit.'

'Yes,' backed up Jo. 'How much riding have you done?'

'Oh, a good bit,' said Helen. 'About the same as you, I suppose. I'm not *very* experienced, but I can trot and canter and jump.' She thought it best not to say that she used to own her own pony and had ridden in a number of Pony Club competitions and gymkhanas. 'Try to make friends slowly,' her mum had said. 'And don't spend all the time telling people about yourself. Find out what they like doing first. You can't expect people to be friends with you if you don't try to be friendly and show an interest in them.'

'How old are you?' said Clare.

'I'm twelve and a half,' replied Helen.

'Well, we're a bit older than you,' said Clare. 'We're thirteen – but I suppose you could tag along – so long as you don't get in the way.'

'Thanks,' said Helen, gratefully. The bell went just then, indicating the end of break time. Jo and Clare walked away together, leaving Helen to follow by herself. Jo felt a bit mean about it, but realised Clare was right, really. Helen seemed so much younger and smaller. If she wasn't up to their standard of riding, they certainly didn't want her holding them up. She could be friends, so long as she knew her place. Helen walked to her desk, pretending not to see anyone. Why was it so hard to make friends, she wondered. I would have thought being interested in riding would have helped. I wish we'd never moved to this town. I wish I was back in Beresford. At least people liked her there. And she had plenty of friends at the riding school back 'home'. She wondered if she would ever stop thinking of Beresford as 'home.'

'Hallo, dear, how did you get on today? Make any friends yet? ' Helen's mum tried not to sound too anxious. She knew how shy Helen was and how hard it was for her to make new friends. She had not wanted to leave Beresford either. But when her husband's job had changed it had affected the whole family. Money was not so plentiful as it had been. They couldn't afford to keep a pony for Helen any more, and Megan, their much loved Welsh Mountain pony had had to be sold – but at least they knew she had gone to a good home. Now Mrs Gray was determined to let Helen ride as much as possible. And, even though it would mean a struggle to find the money, she had booked her into the Own a Pony Week at the new riding school at Manor Farm.

'Well, I tried, Mum. I talked to Jo and Clare – they're going on the Own a Pony Week. They said I could go with them, but I don't really think they want me. They think I'm too small and not a good enough rider – and I'm only twelve.'

'Never mind! At least you've made a start. Why don't we talk to God about it? You know he's interested in all that goes on in our lives.'

'OK.'

Helen and her mum sat on the sofa together. Helen wasn't so sure about God being involved in her life, but Mum believed he heard everything and saw everything that happened. So Helen felt comforted when Mum put her arm round her and prayed. Excited, too. Maybe God *would* do something.

'Dear God,' said Mrs Gray, 'please help Helen to find new friends at school. Show her someone this week who she can help. Amen.'

'Amen,' echoed Helen. Then she looked up, puzzled. 'What do you mean, Mum – I have to find someone I can help? – it's *me* who needs the help!'

'Exactly! But when you stop just thinking about your troubles and try not to feel sorry for yourself, then perhaps you'll find the help *you* need by being a friend to someone else. Other people have problems, too, you know!'

Chapter Two

On Saturday Jo and Clare set off early for the stables. They wanted to be in time to help catch the school ponies and spend as much time as possible with them.

'Come on, you two!' shouted Gail, humping a pile of headcollars into the back of the Land Rover. 'We have to drive down to Long Field today to collect the ponies. You'll have to be quick off the mark next week on the holiday!' Jo and Clare raced across the yard and clambered into the back. Great! They were in time after all!

'Can I ride Barney today, Gail?' asked Jo.

'Oh, and can I have Nelson – *please*!' said Clare.

'We'll see,' smiled Gail, as she changed into second gear through the gate. She liked Jo and Clare and enjoyed teaching them – even though their enthusiasm could be a bit wearing at times! For their part, Jo and Clare thought Gail was the most wonderful instructor in the world – she was the only one they'd ever known!

'You know something?' confided Clare to Jo, 'If I could ride as well as Gail, I'd be satisfied.' Jo nodded in agreement. She was really happy to be here.

'When I leave school,' she said, 'I'm going to get a job in a riding school and be an instructor like Gail.'

When they reached Long Field, Gail and Ted climbed out of the front of the Land Rover. Ted looked after all the stabled horses – mostly liveries (horses and ponies who lived at the stables, but belonged to other people), but he also helped out with the school at weekends and busy holiday times. He was a tough, wiry little man who had spent all his life working with horses. Jo and Clare thought he had been a jockey once, but they weren't sure. He knew a lot about horses, though. He was always calm and gentle with them. 'You be gentle with them,' he'd say, 'and they'll be gentle back. You don't go rushing up to horses like a lunatic. Just approach them quietly.'

Ted rattled the bucket of pony nuts to let the ponies know they'd arrived. Jo and Clare saw eight school ponies grazing at the far end of the field. Eight heads shot up, and eight pairs of eyes stared towards the gate. 'Come on, then,' called Ted, giving the bucket another rattle. 'Have you two got the headcollars?' he added to the girls. Jo and Clare had jumped down from the back of the Land Rover and were untangling the pile of headcollars.

'There's a rope here without a headcollar,' said Clare.

'That's because Pixie is difficult to catch,' said Gail. 'We've left his headcollar on. Don't try to catch him – leave that to Ted or me. If Pixie decides not to be caught today, we could be in for a battle of wills and I don't want to miss the first time!'

They left the bucket outside the field, and each took a handful of pony nuts and a headcollar. Ted said it was safer that way, rather than having several ponies diving their heads into one bucket and fighting over who got the biggest share. By now the ponies had hurried across the field towards them. Jo loved this bit. She watched her beloved Barney as he strode towards them with the others. He was a smart skewbald pony, about 13.2 hands high, with a pretty head and long, unruly mane and tail. Jo slipped the rope round his neck as his nose found the pony nuts in her left hand. Then he tossed away the flies, and wiped the remains of his mouthful on her sleeve as she slipped the headcollar on and fastened it in place. 'Hallo, Barney,' she whispered, 'I hope I get to ride you today.'

'By the time you've finished whispering sweet nothings, we've caught all the rest!' grinned Ted. Everyone knew that Jo was crazy about the brown and white pony. All the ponies were now standing quietly with headcollars in place. Except Pixie, that is. He stood a few yards away watching the proceedings. He wasn't sure whether to come quietly or not. Gail went to collect the bucket and slowly walked towards him. He stretched his neck as far as he could reach, but kept his whole body tense in case he needed to make a dash for it. Everyone held their breath and watched. 'Come on, little one,' said Gail softly. She kept her hands very still as she quietly moved to the pony's side. His own greed persuaded him in the end to lower his head into the bucket and snatch a mouthful of nuts. And as he did so, Gail's fingers quietly closed round the headcollar he was wearing. She let him eat another mouthful, then stroked his neck, and led him over to Ted who clipped the rope in place. Jo saw the pony visibly relax and surrender to being caught. 'I think he's getting better, you know,' said Gail to Ted. 'He's obviously had a bad time somewhere along the line that makes him so hard to catch.'

'I'm sure you're right,' said Ted. 'He just gives in and seems quite OK once he's caught.'

'Be careful how you take the ponies through the gate,' said Ted. 'Don't let them catch their shoulders or hindquarters on the gate posts. And don't let them tread on

14

you!' Jo and Clare led two ponies each, and Ted took four. Gail took the bucket and drove the Land Rover back to the yard ahead of them.

Jo loved being with the ponies. She watched her two as they walked beside her. This was definitely her favourite place in all the world!

As they arrived back at Manor Farm, and the ponies clattered into the yard, Jo and Clare saw a small figure with curly hair coming towards them. It was Helen. Jo felt a pang of conscience. They had said Helen could come with them, but had not done anything about it.

'Here comes that Helen girl,' whispered Clare to Jo, pulling a face.

'I know,' said Jo. 'I'd forgotten all about her.'

'Hallo,' said Helen. 'I was too late to come to the field with you.'

Jo and Clare didn't say anything.

'Here you are, Helen, take a couple of these ponies, will you?' Ted said, handing over two of his ponies to Helen. Jo and Clare were a bit surprised that Ted knew who she was. They watched as she took the two ponies from Ted and led them towards the stalls. It was obvious that she knew how to handle them, as she expertly took them into the right place and tied them up. Jo felt a sense of disappointment – for some reason, she had hoped that Helen wouldn't be able to manage. But then she was suddenly busy with her own two charges, settling them into their places in the stalls and tying them up with the 'quick release knot' used for tying up horses. Jo looked across to see if Helen had used the correct knot with her ponies, and saw that she had. Well, it seems she knows a few basics, she thought to herself. I don't suppose she's much of a rider, though.

Chapter Three

Jo and Clare rode on the first ride. They had spent about half an hour brushing the mud off the ponies, and tacking them up. Gail asked Helen if she would like to help lead one of the ponies for a beginner who had ridden only a few times. Jo and Clare were glad. That was obviously where she belonged – with the beginners! But Helen seemed to be enjoying helping – she was leading Pixie, who, now he was caught and tacked up, turned out to be an ideal beginner's ride. He was gentle and careful, and seemed to know that his rider, Pat, was nervous and not very experienced.

'Helen,' said Gail after a short while, 'would you like to take Pixie into the outside paddock and practise halts, walking on, turns, and trotting – but stay on the leading rein – OK?' Helen nodded and led Pixie away from the others. Jo was surprised that Gail would trust her with a beginner – but then she turned her attention to the ride. Now they would be able to do some cantering and maybe even try a jump. She patted Barney's neck and urged him forward.

'Right, I want the rest of you to take your feet out of stirrups and cross the stirrups in front of your saddles. Sit up straight, Clare,' Gail added. For the next ten minutes the class worked hard, first walking, then trot-

16

ting in changes of rein across the school, and riding twenty metre circles. Jo felt as if her legs would drop off! But she tried hard to sit tall in the saddle, without being stiff, and allowed her legs to hang 'like a dish cloth over the side' as Gail said, and her heels lower than her toes. It was hard work concentrating on keeping the right position. Everyone tried to keep the reins short enough to have a nice even feel on their ponies' mouths, but not too heavy a contact to stop them from moving forward round the school in an orderly sitting trot. 'Don't ride too close,' instructed Gail. 'Remember to keep one pony's distance between you and the next rider.'

For a few minutes all that could be heard was the creak of saddle leather and the even thud of hooves as the ponies trotted round the indoor school. It was a large, airy place, with mirrors down one long side and a viewing gallery at the far end where parents and friends could watch the lessons in progress.

Finally, Gail called the ride to halt, and everyone reached gratefully for their stirrups. Some of the girls lengthened their stirrups. 'That's good,' said Gail, 'at least it shows you're learning to ride longer – which should help you to be more relaxed and more secure as you get *down* into the saddle more.'

The lesson finished with each rider practising moving from trot to canter and back again. Jo struggled with Barney and he kept striking off on the wrong leading leg. He felt very uncomfortable and Jo didn't enjoy riding him as much as she usually did. 'Come on, Jo, you're not really trying!' shouted Gail. 'Use your legs more!' Jo sat down deep in the saddle and dug her heels firmly into Barney's side, but he just responded by running forward into a very fast flying trot: it seemed he was *not* going to oblige with a canter this morning!

Jo was feeling very disgruntled as they untacked the ponies later. 'He was awful!' she said to Clare. 'He just wouldn't do anything right today.'

'You shouldn't blame it all on him,' Gail called out, as she walked by carrying a feed bucket. 'A horse is only as good as its rider, you know!'

Jo was still grumbling about it as the girls ate their sandwiches at lunch time. 'I'd like to see anyone make Barney go well today,' she said.

'Have you seen who's down to ride him at two o'clock?' said Clare.

'No. Who?'

'Helen – who else?'

Jo didn't know whether to be pleased or not. 'Well we'll see how *she* likes being made to look stupid, shan't we?' she said.

'I don't think she'll be able to control him at all,' said Clare.

'Let's go and watch from the visitors' gallery!' suggested Jo.

The ride was in progress as Jo and Clare climbed into the gallery. There were just five horses and ponies moving round the school in a smart trot. Gail made one or two corrections to the riders' positions and then fell silent.

Jo watched Helen on Barney. She could hardly believe it – he was going like a dream! Helen sat perfectly square and balanced in the saddle, and pushed him on to his bit. He moved smoothly from walk, to trot, to canter with perfect precision. He seemed to be answering the slightest aid from Helen, and Jo scowled as Gail kept congratulating her and saying, 'Good! Well done,

Helen!'

Jo didn't like it. Here was Helen riding *her* pony –
and what's more, riding him far better than she could!

Chapter Four

Helen's mum came to collect her later that day. 'Bye,' Helen called out to Jo and Clare. 'See you on Monday at school.' But Jo and Clare didn't feel like being friendly and turned the other way.

'Are those the two friends you told me about?' Helen's mum asked as she got into the car. 'They don't seem very friendly to me!'

'Oh, I can't help that, Mum,' said Helen. 'I've tried but they just don't want to know.' Then she turned and smiled at her mother. 'But you know what happened today? I *did* find someone else who needed help and we've made friends. I wasn't *really* sure whether to believe in God or not, but I decided to give it a try – to really look for an answer: and there it was! So now I know God cares about me and will help me – even to make friends!'

'That's *good*,' said Mum. 'What happened exactly?'

'Well, Gail asked me to take this beginner – called Pat – on a leading rein, and I just showed her how to sit properly, how to hold the reins and use her legs and so on. Then at the end of the lesson when everyone was untacking the ponies she got in a terrible muddle because she undid all the wrong bits on the bridle – you know, she undid the cheek pieces and reins instead of the throat lash and noseband, and the whole bridle fell to bits! She was really upset about it at first and nearly cried. But then I showed her how to put it all together again and we laughed about it. We've spent the rest of the day together and she's coming on the Own a Pony Week next week, so we've decided to help each other again then. Do you think we could invite her round for tea sometime?'

'I'm sure we could,' said Mrs Gray. 'That would be lovely.'

'Anyway,' Helen rattled on, 'I've decided it *is* worth believing in God, now that he's answered that prayer and found me a friend. So I'm going to believe in him myself from now on. What do you think I should ask him for next?'

'Hey – hold on a minute! God isn't some kind of heavenly Father Christmas just waiting for us to ask him for things. He wants us to know him as a friend, and to love him.'

'I don't really know what you mean. How can a person really *know* God like a friend? No one ever sees him, do they? If he's invisible, how can you know him?'

'It is difficult. But that's why Jesus came to earth in the first place – to show people what God is like. Jesus is God – and getting to know Jesus is really the only way you can know God.'

'But Jesus lived a long time ago, didn't he? And he died – so how can you know him now?'

'That's right – Jesus did die, but he came alive again and is alive today. When we prayed the other day, we were praying to a living God, not a dead one. Look, think about how you felt when you tried to make friends with Jo and Clare and they didn't want to know. You went to them, and they turned away – right?'

'Yes, I know. I felt awful. But I don't feel so bad now that I've made friends with Pat.'

'Exactly. When Jesus came to earth lots of people just didn't want to know. They turned away and refused to have anything to do with him. But those who *did* believe that Jesus had come from God trusted him and loved him. They became friends.'

'I thought you could just pray and ask for things – like we did.'

'Yes, of course you can do that. But there's more to a friendship than just asking for favours, isn't there?'

'I suppose so. But how do you actually get to be a friend of Jesus, then?'

'How did you get to be a friend of Pat's?'

'Well, I was looking for someone to be friends with, and we had been together all morning and had a good laugh together over her bridle-in-bits – it was just nice having each other and we both said we'd meet up again on the riding holiday next week. That's all!'

'Well, all you have to do is to ask Jesus to be with you – thank him for wanting you as a friend. It's as simple as that!'

Mrs Gray drew up outside their house and she and Helen went inside.

'Before you do anything else, young lady, off with the dirty boots, and upstairs and get cleaned up. There's plenty of hot water so you can soak yourself in the bath – I don't want you smelling of horses all evening!'

Helen lay back in the warm water, enjoying the comfort and sweet steaminess of the bath. Perhaps she could talk to Jesus now. 'Jesus,' she said out loud, then looked round at the door, just to make sure that no one would overhear and think she was stupid, or talking to herself. 'Jesus, if you *are* really here, even though I can't see you, I do want to be your friend. I'm not really sure yet what it all means, but I want to understand. I know how hard it is when people don't like you – like Jo and Clare – but you had that, too, didn't you? – people who hated you. Thanks for helping me to make friends with Pat, by the way. And thanks for a super day.'

Jo and Clare didn't have such a happy end to their day. They went home together on their bikes and didn't speak much until they came to Foley Hill, where they both dismounted as it was too steep to ride up. 'You know, it's all right for that Helen girl,' muttered Clare. 'Posh car to go home in. She makes me sick!'

'She managed to ride Barney, though, didn't she? That makes me feel even sicker. Why didn't she say she was such a great rider? Just so that she could show off all the more, I suppose,' Jo answered her own question, and kicked a loose stone as they plodded up the hill together.

'If she thinks she's going to ride in the gymkhana at the end of the Own a Pony Week and win everything, she's got another think coming!' said Clare, angrily.

'I wonder how we could stop her, though?' said Jo. 'Gail seems to think she's so good – she even let her take that beginner during our lesson this morning. Did you see her?'

'Well, we'll think of something, we've got the whole of next week at school first. She'll be sorry she came here at all by the time we've finished with her!'

'Hope she breaks a leg!' Jo said finally.

Jo knew she didn't actually mean that, of course – not *really* – but it felt better having said it. They both reached the top of Foley Hill and remounted.

'Come on – race you home!' said Clare, 'let's forget

about snooty little Helen!'

Both girls sped off for home. Jo wouldn't admit it – not even to Clare – but she felt uncomfortable and a bit guilty about Helen. But she soon shrugged the feeling off as she pedalled hard in pursuit of her friend. She wasn't going to let the new girl spoil things – she liked them just the way they were!

Chapter Five

The next day was Sunday, and Helen and her mum usually went to church together. Dad came too, when he was not at work. Helen liked it best when they all went, especially as this was a new church, and, like school, it wasn't easy making new friends.

'Mum, I'm looking forward to going today,' she said, 'now that I'm thinking about God and believing in him for myself.' The truth was that, although Helen didn't mind going to church, it was a bit boring sometimes. But now perhaps it would be different. She had once tried to read the Bible for herself, but it was hard to understand and she'd given up after a little while. Some of the words were long and difficult, and it seemed they often meant something other than what they said! However, this morning she took her Good News Bible, and actually began to listen to the preacher as he spoke about Jesus and what it meant to be a Christian. He was talking about how Jesus had made friends with a woman by a well, when he asked her for a drink of water. The woman was shunned by many of the people in her town, and she had to sneak out in the hot midday sun, when everyone else was resting indoors. That was the time that no one would see her. She was afraid of their cold stares and taunts and tried to keep out of their way. She was really surprised to see Jesus sitting by the well, and even more surprised when he showed he wanted to talk to her and be friends!

Helen thought of the struggle she was having at school – and at the stables – with Jo and Clare. She thought about the way they had ignored her and given her cold stares. It *was* nice having Pat for a friend, and she was glad about that. But she was still unhappy that Jo and Clare showed they obviously didn't like her or want to be friends. It wasn't easy to be friendly towards them when they were like that. She had said she didn't care what they thought, but she knew that she did really. It would be so much better all round if she could find a way to be friends.

'. . . and that's how Jesus was able to make friends with the woman at the well,' the man in the pulpit was saying. 'And God helped her to tell other people about Jesus in such a wonderful way.' Helen came to with a start, and realised she had missed most of what he had been saying because she had been busy thinking about her own problems – again! Would she ever be able to concentrate and learn about Jesus properly? She sneaked a glance sideways at Mum and Dad. They seemed to be listening OK. Why did her mind wander off like that when everyone else seemed to be able to listen? Helen stood up to join in the closing song. But she wasn't even thinking about the words she was singing. She was busy telling herself off for having missed most of the morning's sermon. Was it really this difficult to take in what was being said? Maybe she wouldn't be able to keep it up after all. What was the use if she couldn't even listen?

Helen was still feeling fed up with herself as they made their way out towards the morning sunshine. In the entrance to the church was a bookstall and a small carpeted area where young children played in a crèche during the service. Several mothers were chatting together, and a few people stepped over various dolls and bricks and other toys to reach the bookstall.

'We could do with a bit more space, couldn't we?' laughed one of the mothers as she rescued her baby from the pathway of Helen's dad, who was trying to make his way through to the books without treading on any toys or infants.

'You're new here, aren't you?' continued the mother, now holding her baby, and rocking him quickly from side to side. The baby stared at Helen and watched her as he swung backwards and forwards in his mother's arms. Helen stared back, and smiled.

'Yes, we are,' her dad was saying. 'We moved here from Beresford a few weeks back. I'm Bob, and this is my wife, Mary. And this is our daughter, Helen.'

'It's nice to meet you,' said the mother. 'I'm June. And this bundle of trouble is Michael.' She stopped her frantic rocking of the baby and he reached out his hand to Helen.

'He likes you!' smiled June. 'Just give him a finger to hang on to and you'll be friends for life!'

Helen laughed and obediently offered her hand. Michael's tiny, sticky fingers closed round one of hers and held on tight. She was surprised what a strong grip he had.

'Why don't you come down to our young people's meeting this afternoon?' said June to Helen. 'They have a meeting for people your age called ETF – stands for Eleven-to-Fifteen – every Sunday afternoon and it would be a good way of getting to know some of them.'

'Seems like a good idea, Helen,' said her mum.

'What do they do exactly?' asked Helen, hesitantly.

'Oh, all sorts of things. Very informal,' said June. 'Sometimes they play table tennis, or board games, or just sit around and chat. Sometimes they organise other outings during the week and go swimming or ice skating. When it's here on a Sunday afternoon they usually have a discussion or talk about being a Christian. In fact,' she rushed on without pausing for breath, 'today would be a good day for you to start, as they're all going in the minibus down to the coast. On sunny days like today, they sometimes do that – take a picnic, have their meeting on the beach, and maybe play some games. My two usually go, and love it – you could go with them.'

Helen looked puzzled.

'Oh, not Michael!' laughed June. 'I have twins who are older – Jeremy and Pat. In fact, they're over there, talking to Dave.'

Helen and her parents looked across to where June nodded her head.

'I know,' grinned June, in answer to an unvoiced question. 'There's a big gap between the twins and Michael, but that's a long story!'

But Helen wasn't listening – she stared across to where the twins stood.

'It's Pat!' she said, in amazement. 'Mum – that's my friend Pat from the riding school!'

Chapter Six

'I didn't know you were a twin,' said Helen.

'I didn't know you came to this church!' said Pat.

'I didn't – I mean, we've only just started. Is this your church, then?'

The two girls were delighted to see each other, and soon they had arranged to go together to the ETF meeting.

'We're going down to the sea this afternoon,' said Pat. 'Will you be able to get back here in time? The minibus leaves at three.'

Helen smiled and nodded. 'It sounds terrific!'

Somehow Helen was surprised to find that Pat was a Christian. It was great to find the *same* friend in two places!

'You look very different – not wearing your riding stuff, I mean,' said Helen.

'So do you!' said Pat. 'That's really good, isn't it? We can be friends at the riding school as well as here! Have you been a Christian a long time?'

Helen was a bit taken aback.

'Well, I suppose . . . no, not really. In fact, er, last night. When I got home, I talked to Jesus then – in the bath,' she added a bit sheepishly. Both girls laughed.

'I don't suppose he minded!' grinned Pat. 'Come on

– I'll show you the downstairs hall where we usually meet – when we're not on trips out, that is!'

Later that day, Helen joined Pat and Jeremy and the others as they piled into the back of the church's mini-bus. There were twelve from the youth group and two leaders – Dave and his wife, Ann.

'Good thing no one else turned up, or they'd have had to run behind!' said Ann, climbing over several pairs of legs, so she could sit with Pat and Helen. Dave checked that the back door was securely locked, then heaved himself into the driver's seat.

'Anyone who turns up now will be left behind!' he said, and leaned forward to turn the ignition key. 'Here we go – look out Sandy Bay!'

'This is your first time with this mob, isn't it?' Ann asked Helen. Helen struggled not to feel shy, but just managed to smile and say 'yes'.

Pat didn't suffer from shyness.

'This is my friend, Helen,' she said to Ann. 'We go riding together. Ann and Dave are our Great and Wonderful Leaders!' she grinned to Helen. 'We do everything they say!'

'That'll be the day!' laughed Ann. 'Let me know when you've started will you, so I don't miss it!'

Then, to Helen, she said, 'It's really nice to have you, Helen. Hope you survive the day!' Then she moved back up the bus to sit with Dave at the front. Pat and Helen talked non-stop. Helen had almost forgotten Jo and Clare and the misery she had felt about them earlier. She liked being with Pat and her twin brother. Jeremy didn't share his sister's love of riding, but he was friendly enough, and smiled at Helen and said it was good that she had joined them.

It wasn't long before they arrived at the coast, parked the minibus in a car-park on top of the cliffs, and piled out into the afternoon sunshine. The sea lay far below them, with large, overhanging cliffs stretching to the right and left, as far as the eye could see. As they stood looking down to the beach below, they could see several tiny coves, each divided by small outcrops of rocks jutting out into the sea. It was not too difficult to scramble from one cove to the next over the pile of rocks, although you had to be careful not to get cut off by the tide when the sea was on its way in. Some of the coves did not have steps leading down to the sands, and sometimes people had had to be rescued because they'd been trapped by the tide.

'Let's go down to this bay here,' said Ann. 'We can have it to ourselves.' The bay next to the one Ann pointed to was already occupied by a group who had spread themselves out and were obviously enjoying a quiet picnic.

'They won't want to be disturbed by our crowd!' said Jeremy. 'Anyway, they've got a dog with them and I expect he'll be a nuisance when we play cricket.'

The way down to the beach was a steep set of stone steps – no obstacle to this bunch of healthy blue jeans, and they were soon at the bottom of the cliffs in their own 'private place' as Pat called it.

'Let's set up shop here,' said Dave, dumping the various bags and boxes he was carrying – not to mention his guitar in its battered case. Jeremy had brought a cricket bat, but forgotten the stumps, so they used the cliff face as a wicket.

'Saves us having to have a wicket keeper,' said one of the boys. Most of the group joined in the friendly cricket match, though one or two wandered off to look for crabs or shells which had been marooned in the rock pools. Ann covered herself in suntan lotion and stretched out on a blanket, determined to make the most of trying to get a suntan on this half-day visit to the sea!

About an hour later, everyone was ready for a break, and gladly responded to Dave's shout, 'Drinks Is Served!'

'Come on,' said Pat to Helen, 'if you don't grab one quick, all the Coke goes and you're left with the squash!'

Everyone helped themselves to a drink and sandwiches or sausage rolls. It was amazing how starving hungry you could get after just one game of cricket. Some of the group sprawled out on the sands, while others perched precariously on jutting pieces of rock, or sat on a bit of Ann's blanket. 'This is the "God Slot",' whispered Pat to Helen. 'When we're back at the church we sometimes watch a video, or we have a discussion. But when we're outside like this, we usually sing some songs and Dave talks a bit.' She was enjoying explaining everything to Helen.

Dave tuned up his guitar and then looked round at them all.

'OK – settle down everybody. We're just going to try a couple of new choruses.' There were groans from the unmusical ones, but most of them joined in, in a good natured way, and enjoyed learning the two-part songs. Helen knew one of the songs from her other church, so she felt even more at home. 'I know this one,' she whispered to Pat.

After the singing, Dave announced that there would be a barbecue on Tuesday evening instead of the afternoon meeting next Sunday. Helen felt a quick moment of embarrassment as he welcomed her and another girl who had come for the first time.

'For those who are here for the first time – and any who've forgotten! – we're in the middle of looking at some Psalms,' said Dave. 'Who can bring us up to date with what we've discovered so far?'

Various people mentioned different things that they had discussed in previous weeks, and Dave wrote down the points on a large card he had propped up against a rock. 'He has to have a visual aid, no matter what!' whispered Pat to Helen. Dave's writing was not exactly easy to read, but no one seemed to mind. After a few minutes, the card was full of comments like 'God is the creator of the earth' . . . 'God is a shepherd' . . . 'God can hear when we talk to him' . . . 'God can speak to us'.

'OK – hold it there,' said Dave. 'Now we're going to look at Psalm 139. I know you haven't got Bibles with you today, so you'll just have to listen.'

Dave talked about how God was everywhere and knew everything about them – even the tiniest detail.

'There's no place you can go,' he said, 'where God is not. Some people have tried to hide away from God by sailing over the seas' (pointing to the sea), 'or hiding in caves' (pointing to the rocks), 'but this Psalm tells us that God is everywhere and knows all about us. And he loves us, no matter what we do. No one can get so bad, or so far away from God, that he will stop caring. *You* might stop loving God, but *he* will never stop loving you.' Then Dave read from the beginning of the psalm: 'You know when I sit and when I rise . . .'

'That's for when you're doing a rising trot!' hissed Pat to Helen.

Much of what Dave said next was lost on them as they both giggled at their own joke. But Helen thought about the talk later.

'God is everywhere,' Dave's words played themselves over again in her mind. '*You* might stop loving God, but *he* will never stop loving you.'

Wouldn't it be nice, Helen thought to herself, if Jo and Clare could know about God as well? I wish we didn't have to hate each other all the time. Helen sighed. Well, it seemed that was the way they wanted it – if they didn't want to be friends, it was their fault, not hers.

Chapter Seven

'Jo? It's Clare here.'

Jo had slept in, as it was Sunday morning, and she had nothing in particular to get up for.

'Oh, hallo, Clare,' she yawned into the phone. 'I'm not really awake yet. Whatever are you ringing this early for?'

'It's not early – lazybones! It's nearly ten thirty! Listen – we're going on a picnic and Mum says would you like to come – if you can wake up, that is!'

'Cheek! Of course I can! That'll be great. I haven't got anything planned for today. I'll have to find my mum, though. I'm not even sure where she is. This place is deserted. I expect she's in the garden or somewhere. But I'm sure it'll be all right. Shall I come round to your house? What time?'

'Can you make it by about eleven? We're going down to the sea – bring your swimming things, we might even get a chance to go in. And Whistler's coming too.'

Whistler was Clare's dog. He managed to go with Jo and Clare just about everywhere, and they both liked him. He was the next best thing to having your own pony, Clare said. Whistler was a mongrel-of-mongrels. Almost any breed of dog could be seen in him. Clare's dad said he was mostly sheepdog, but related to Queen

Anne, because his front paws turned out at the end of long brown legs, and looked like the bent legs on Queen Anne furniture. Clare and her mother both said he definitely had some terrier in him, because of his tendency to fight every other male dog he met, and fall in love with every female dog. And Jo said he reminded her of a spaniel or a labrador, because he had lovely brown eyes and always made a beeline for water given half the chance of a swim or even a paddle. The prospect of a picnic by the sea with Whistler could be a wet one! But it would be fun, and Jo thought she could do with some of that!

'Sure! I'll be there!' said Jo. 'By the way, do I need to bring anything – food, I mean?'

'No, of course not. Mum'll see to that. Don't forget a towel, though, with your swimming gear.'

'OK, thanks. See you later.'

Jo hung up, and looked out of the window to see if her mother was anywhere in sight.

'Wonder where she is?' she muttered to herself. 'I'd better get a move on. Where on earth is my swimming coz?'

Jo hurried upstairs and quickly washed and rummaged round for shirt and jeans. A lightning search through her drawers and cupboards eventually found her swimming costume, which she stuffed into a bag, and then she went to find a large towel in the airing cupboard. She heard the kitchen door open. She hurried out of her bedroom and leaned over the banister.

'Mum! Is that you? Clare's been on the phone and invited me to a picnic – now. Is it OK for me to go?'

Jo's mother had been working in the garden, and was busy scrubbing the dirt from her hands.

'That depends on where you're going and who with,'

she said. 'Come down here and talk about it properly.'

Jo raced downstairs, two at a time, and hurried into the kitchen.

'Everyone's going,' she said. 'Clare and her mum and dad – they're taking all the food. And Whistler's coming, too. We're going to the seaside – and is it all right if I swim? Clare's allowed to,' she added, as she read the look on her mother's face.

'All right, then,' she said. 'But just a minute – have you had anything to eat?'

Jo was about ten minutes late by the time she reached Clare's house.

'Sorry,' she said. 'Mum insisted that I ate some breakfast first.'

Everyone piled into the car. Clare's mum and dad were in the front, and Jo and Clare shared the back seat with Whistler. He stood between them, refusing to sit down, and waving his long plumy tail first in Clare's face, then in Jo's.

'He pongs a bit, doesn't he?' whispered Jo to Clare.

'You wait till he's been in the water – it's even worse then!' grinned Clare. She grabbed hold of his tail and tried to make him sit, but it was no good. Whistler was enjoying the ride, and had planted his Queen Anne legs firmly and squarely on the seat, and had no intention of moving until they reached the end of their journey.

An hour later they arrived at the coast, and parked in the cliff top car-park, overlooking the sea. Whistler was so excited by the time the car door opened that he was promptly sick just as everyone piled out into the car-park. Clare and Jo pulled a face at the disgusting sight and smell, and Clare's mum dragged the dog away from the car.

'I knew we shouldn't have given him any breakfast!'

she said.

'I'm just glad he got out of the car first!' said Clare's dad. 'Come on, I expect we'll all feel better after some fresh air and exercise.'

Everyone helped to carry chairs and towels and various bags laden with food and drink and Mum's knitting and Dad's newspaper. Whistler seemed very pleased with himself and glad to be in action once more. Clare's mum had a quick look round to make sure no other dogs were in sight, then slipped off his lead and watched him charge ahead of his little party down the rough stone steps which led to the beach. Whenever they came here for a day, they always made for the quieter end of town as not many people seemed to know about these bays with their smooth sand and sheltering craggy cliffs. Next to the stables, this was Jo's favourite place. Whistler had now reached the bottom of the steps and turned to look back at his family carefully coming down towards him. He set off, back up the steps again with great speed and enthusiasm to chase in circles round them and bark his delight at being free to run to his heart's content.

'There! Didn't I always say he's a sheepdog?' said Clare's dad. 'Rounding up comes natural to a dog like him. We're his flock and he's come to collect us up! Shame about his legs!' This last remark was for Clare's benefit, as she always defended Whistler and didn't like to see anything less than perfection in him. She objected strongly when her dad teased her and made rude remarks about Whistler's 'Queen Anne legs'.

'There's nothing wrong with his legs!' she said. 'Anyway, he's *not* a sheepdog, he's a terrier!'

'I hope you two aren't going to argue all day!' said Clare's mum. 'Jo and I have come here for a bit of peace and quiet, haven't we, Jo?'

Jo grinned, but said nothing. She liked being with Clare's family and enjoyed the banter and the way they teased each other in a harmless, fun sort of way. She helped to set out the rugs and chairs on the beach and carefully placed the bag of food she was carrying in the shade of some rocks that jutted above where they were sitting.

'Are you two going for a swim?' said Clare's mum. 'Don't be too long, then we can eat.'

'Come on, Jo! Race you in!' said Clare. 'Whistler's already been in – and out!'

She pointed to where the dog had chased into the waves and galloped out again and now stood near the water's edge, shaking himself, before turning to rush back in for more.

'Don't know why he bothers to shake!' laughed Jo.

She and Clare were soon changed and running down the tiny beach to join the delighted Whistler and enjoy the salty cold water as it lazily splashed into the bay, as if it had almost forgotten to wash into this tiny cove.

It was too cold to stay in for long, and, in any case, Jo and Clare were hungry. After about twenty minutes, they were happy to leave the water and make their way back to where Clare's parents sat waiting for them, surrounded by welcoming towels and masses of food.

'I'm absolutely starving!' said Clare, rubbing herself hard with her towel.

'Me too!' said Jo. 'I can never decide which makes me hungrier – riding or swimming. I know which I like best, though!'

'So do I!' said Clare.

Clare's mum was busy unwrapping parcels of sandwiches and home made pie, packets of crisps and apples and bananas. Enough to satisfy the biggest of appetites!

Everyone was hungry, and soon devoured the good food she had prepared.

'John, could you pour out the drinks, please? There's a flask of coffee or the girls might prefer cold – in the bottle in the yellow bag.'

Clare's dad carefully balanced four flask tops on the tiny camping stool, and poured out the various drinks.

'Just look at Whistler,' said Clare, 'don't you think he'd make a great horse?'

Whistler had followed the girls out of the water and given himself a good shake before rolling over in the warm sand. Now he trotted towards them waving his long tail behind him like a flag.

'He's a bit too long in the back to make a good riding horse,' said Clare's dad, just to show that he knew about these things. 'And as for his legs . . .'

'Dad! Do you have to? If you think he'd make such a rotten horse, why can't you buy me one? . . . not even a horse – a pony would do. Nelson, for instance!'

Clare was always reminding her parents that she would like a pony of her own, but she knew there was no chance of that, so didn't wait for a reply.

'When I grow up and marry my millionaire,' she said, 'then I'll have hundreds of horses and ponies all to myself!'

'Wouldn't it be nice,' said Jo, 'to have a pony of your very own?'

'I'm getting bored with all this horse talk,' said Clare's dad. 'Why don't you two take Whistler for a walk? See if you can get round to the next bay and back before the tide comes in.'

'Is that safe, John?' said Clare's mum, looking up from her knitting.

'Yes, course it is!' answered Clare, not waiting for her

father to speak. 'Anyway, there's steps up the next cove as well, so we'll be fine. Come on, Jo – race you to the other side!'

Jo and Clare ran down the beach, followed by a delighted Whistler, who was soon racing ahead of them, pleased at the prospect of more action. The girls clambered over the rocks, and made their way round the headland to reach the next bay.

'Jo!' said Clare, suddenly grabbing hold of her friend's arm. 'Do you see what I see?'

Jo followed Clare's gaze, and gasped in astonishment. 'It can't be! That's Pat and . . .'

'And snooty Helen!' finished Clare. 'I don't believe it! Who would have thought that *she* would be here?'

'Who's the crowd they're with?' asked Jo.

'Not sure. I think it's that lot from the church – do you think *they* go to church?' Clare curled up her nose in disgust. 'Might have known. We can't even get away from her on a day out.'

'I hope they don't come round to *our* beach!' said Jo. 'That would spoil everything.'

'She spoils everything anyway,' said Clare. 'Let's go back. I don't want to see her – not when I don't have to.'

They made their way back across the rocks, not wanting any of the church youth group to see them.

'You know,' said Clare, 'I've been thinking. We ought to just teach her a lesson. She's spoiled everything, hasn't she? At school and at the stables. Why don't we send her to Coventry? We could get some of the girls in our class to do it with us, then perhaps she'll get the message and just leave us alone.'

'What do you mean – send her to Coventry?'

'That's when everyone makes a pact not to talk to

41

someone. If we send her to Coventry for a day, no one talks to her for a whole day – or week – or as long as we decide. Could be forever!'

'She's certainly becoming a pain!' said Jo.

'Let's do it then!' said Clare. 'It'll be a bit of fun – and I'm just fed up of having her hanging around everywhere we go. She's so high-and-mighty. We won't say anything to Mum and Dad, though, eh?'

'OK,' said Jo. 'We'll send her to Coventry – but just for a day.'

Chapter Eight

'Where's Whistler?' asked Clare's mother. Jo and Clare had been so busy making plans to send Helen to Coventry, that they hadn't noticed that the dog was not with them as they made their way back to Clare's parents.

'Whistler? Oh no! I thought he was following us!' Clare looked all round, but he was nowhere in sight.

'He must have stayed round the other side!' said Jo.

'Well, you'd better go and bring him back,' said Clare's dad. 'You know what a wanderer he can be!'

Jo and Clare looked at each other and pulled a face. There was nothing for it but to go back to the headland and look for him.

'Stupid dog!' grumbled Clare.

'He's probably gone to join the church choir!' said Jo, trying to joke about the situation, but Clare was too cross to appreciate it.

'Why do we have to have a dog who's always wandering off after other people and dogs and things? I hope we can get him without *her* seeing us.'

They climbed over the rocks until they could see the youth group at the far side of the bay. They were in the middle of a game of cricket and Whistler had gone to help by chasing the ball. He was a good fielder, but hadn't quite got the hang of returning the ball afterwards, and thought it was great fun to be chased by four or five players trying to retrieve the ball, while the batsman delightedly kept making more and more runs.

'Eh! Is this your dog?' shouted one of the boys, as he spotted Jo and Clare. 'Come and get him, will you, he's ruining our match!'

'No he's not!' laughed the batsman, 'he's doing a great job!'

'Whistler! Come here! Heel!' shouted Clare. 'I'll wring his neck!' she muttered under her breath. 'Why does he have to be so disobedient?'

'Why did he have to join *them* of all people?' said Jo. 'Whistler – come here!'

But Whistler had no intention of even noticing them. He was having too much fun, and the more he was chased, the more he liked it. Soon everyone was joining in, and all except Jo and Clare thoroughly enjoyed trying to catch the dog as he charged in and out of the crowd. He hadn't had such a good game for ages! It was finally a superb rugby dive from Jeremy that ended the proceedings, as he flung himself at the dog and managed to grab first the long hair round his neck and then take a firm hold of his collar. Once caught, Whistler stood there, panting and waving his tail, feeling thoroughly pleased with himself.

Clare took hold of his collar and made him sit.

'You're a *bad* dog!' she scolded angrily.

'How did you get here?' said Jeremy. 'I didn't see you coming down the steps.'

'We didn't,' said Jo. 'We climbed over the rocks at the headland and came round from the next bay.'

'Hallo!' said Pat and Helen, who had walked over to see what was going on.

'Hallo,' said Jo.

'Come on, we've got to be going,' said Clare, ignoring them.

'Would you like a drink of squash – or a biscuit? I think there's some left,' said Jeremy, trying to be friendly.

Jo looked at the crowd around her, and thought how good it might be to belong to a group like this. They all seemed to be having such a great time. She wanted to say 'thank you' and accept Jeremy's offer of a drink. But then she looked at Helen and shook her head.

'No thanks,' she said.

'We've got to be going,' said Clare again. 'Come on, Jo.'

Clare turned, without a backwards glance, and walked off towards the headland, dragging a reluctant Whistler with her. She wished she had a lead so that she didn't have to walk in this ridiculous, bent over fashion, but she knew if she let go of his collar, the chase would start all over again. She felt angry with Jo for even saying hallo to Helen and Pat. 'I do believe she would even have accepted a drink from them!' she said to Whistler, who was not really listening, as he was busy trying to keep up with his mistress as she dragged him across the beach. Clare wanted Jo's friendship to herself, and didn't mean to share it with anyone else. Amazing, she thought to herself, how *she* (meaning Helen) always manages to spoil everything! Well, I'll show her. She won't be so friendly after everyone at school has sent her to Coventry!

Chapter Nine

Helen let the door slam shut behind her. She dumped her case on the kitchen table and slumped into the nearest chair.

'I'm glad this is the last week of the term!' she said. 'Today has been awful!'

'Not more trouble with Jo and Clare?' asked Helen's mum.

'They're really horrible! I just wish they weren't going on the riding holiday next week. I still don't know what I've done to them, but they just go out of their way to be nasty. And *don't* tell me to pray about it,' she added. 'I've tried that. Nothing seems to work.'

Helen's mother said nothing. She was not happy about the situation either, and she had been praying that things would get better, but she had to admit that they hadn't. For some reason, Jo and Clare seemed to have it in for Helen, and she was at a loss as to what to do.

'Well, at least you had a good time at the youth club yesterday afternoon. Maybe you should forget about Jo and Clare and just get on with being friends with Pat.'

'That's all very well,' said Helen. 'Pat doesn't go to my school – and *they* do.'

'Couldn't you and Pat invite them to the youth club?'

Helen snorted and pulled a face.

'You must be kidding!' she said. 'If I mentioned church or anything like that, it would just give them an excuse to laugh and make things even worse. They just hate me and that's all there is to it.'

'Well, never mind that for now,' said Helen's mother, trying to change the subject, 'can you help me get tea ready?'

'No I *can't*!' answered Helen, rudely. 'I don't *want* any tea!' She snatched up her case and banged out of the kitchen. She slammed her bedroom door this time, and threw herself on to her bed.

'Why does everything have to go wrong?' she said, angrily, and thumped the pillow hard. She thought back over the day and relived the awful moment when she had gone into the second lesson that morning. Jo and Clare had been standing with a group of girls in the corner of the room whispering together. As soon as they saw Helen, everyone stopped talking, and moved away. One or two glanced at her and sniggered, but no one spoke. As the morning wore on, Helen soon discovered that she was 'in Coventry', and there was a conspiracy of silence against her. No one said anything, and if she tried to speak to one of them, they made no reply and stared beyond her, as if she wasn't there. It was obvious that Jo and Clare had set the whole thing up, and all Helen could do was keep to herself, and long for the day to end. Now it had ended. But there was still tomorrow. And the day after that. How was she going to get through? She leaned over and picked up the Bible that lay on the bedside table. It was such a big book, she thought, how could she begin to read it? Dave had said that God would help you and speak to you as you read it – but where to begin? And how could God speak anyway? Were you supposed to hear a voice, or what?

She found the place in Psalms where they had read the Bible in the youth group the day before. As she flicked over the pages, she read some words which seemed to describe how she was feeling. 'I ask the Lord for help. I tell him all my troubles. When I am ready to give up, he knows what I should do. In the past where I walk, my enemies have hidden a trap for me. When I look beside me, I see that there is no one to help me, no one to protect me. No one cares for me.'

'That just about sums it up,' she said out loud. 'Maybe I'll try praying. Jesus, please will you help me? Show me what to do. I really don't know how to make friends with Jo and Clare. I have tried! And now everyone at school is against me, too. Please show me – I'm not really sure what Dave means when he says you speak to people as they read the Bible. I don't know which bit to read – it's so big! Please show me.'

There was a page at the front of Helen's Bible which listed various subjects and where to find them, and she looked there, hoping to discover some words that would help. As her eyes scanned down the list of headings, she read one that said 'What to do about anger', and suddenly felt a jab of guilt – not against Jo and Clare, but about how she had flared up in anger just now against her mother, and stormed upstairs. Helen found the verses in the 5th chapter of Matthew, and read: 'If you are about to offer your gift to God and there you remember that your brother has something against you, leave your gift, go at once and make peace with your brother, and then come back and offer your gift to God.' There it was in black and white! Not the kind of answer she was looking for, but Helen knew, as surely as if the words had been spoken out loud, what she had to do. She needed to say sorry to Mum, and put things right with her before she could expect God to answer any more prayers. Oh, why was it always so hard to say sorry? 'OK, Lord,' she said out loud. 'I'll go and say sorry to Mum. Please help me.'

Helen made her way downstairs. Her mother was finishing preparing tea. She looked up as Helen entered. She looked tired and a bit fed up herself. She opened her mouth to speak, but Helen butted in before she could say anything.

'Mum, I'm sorry for dashing out like that. I . . . well, I . . . er . . . can I do anything to help?' Helen had meant to tell her mother about how God had spoken to her as she had read the Bible, but she suddenly found it difficult. Instead she said, 'I'm sorry I lost my temper.'

'That's all right,' said her mother. 'Tea's just about ready now. Why don't you wash your hands and come and eat?'

'Yes, OK – but there's something I have to do first. Won't be a minute. I *am* sorry, Mum,' she said again, wanting to be sure that her mother had really heard and everything was right between them. After all, that was the agreement – she would 'put things right' by saying sorry, then God would speak to her again and show her what to do about Jo and Clare. Helen held on to the door, and looked back at her mother to see her reaction.

'All right, dear,' said her mum.

Then she looked up and saw Helen looking at her. She smiled at her daughter.

'I forgive you,' she said. 'Not easy saying sorry, is it? Go on then – don't be long!'

Back in the privacy of her own room, Helen sat on her bed. She picked up the Bible again, and began to feel excited.

'Well, I did it, Lord,' she said. 'I made it right with Mum before coming back to you. Now please tell me what to do about Jo and Clare.'

She turned up the page at the beginning again where
the various subjects were listed. She felt quite pleased
with herself when her finger ran down the list and she
read 'What to do about anger'. 'I've done that!' she said,
and read on as her finger travelled down the page. Then
she saw the words 'What to do about enemies'. Amazing!
God was going to tell her after all! She couldn't quite
work out why she was surprised to see it spelt out so
clearly. Did she, or did she not expect God to speak?
He'd done it the first time, so why be surprised when
he did it again? The verses this time were in Luke, and
it took her a bit longer to find it. Matthew, she knew,
was easy, as that was the first book in the New Testa-
ment. She found the verses in Luke chapter 6 and read:
'Love your enemies, do good to those who hate you,
bless those who curse you, pray for those who ill-treat
you.'

Helen closed the Bible quickly.

She felt that was a bit much – a bit below the belt!
She'd already done one hard thing – saying sorry to
Mum – now it seemed God expected her to do something
even harder!

'Helen! Are you coming for your tea or not?'

Mum's voice broke in on her thoughts, and she was
glad of an excuse to leave things as they were. She wasn't
quite ready yet to pray for Jo and Clare. That was asking
a bit too much.

'Just coming, Mum,' she called out, and, leaving her
Bible on the bed, she went downstairs.

Mum had dished up home made pizza for tea, with
green and red peppers and ham and mushrooms steam-
ing on top of a delicious tomato and cheese base.

'There's a barbecue tomorrow evening for the ETF

group – do you think I could go?' Helen asked, between mouthfuls.

'I don't see why not,' said Mrs Gray. 'Is Pat going to be there?'

'Not sure. I expect so.'

Helen hadn't really thought about Pat. She did think it would be a good idea to talk to Dave, though. Perhaps she would be able to tell him about how she had read the Bible and how God had spoken to her. And what did you do when God told you to do something that was too difficult? How could you love your enemies and pray for them, when they were so horrible?

Chapter Ten

The next day at school didn't seem quite so bad. Some of the girls who had joined in 'sending Helen to Coventry' the day before had got bored with it, and forgot that they were supposed to be ignoring her. And, now that Helen was looking forward to the barbecue that evening, she didn't mind being on her own. Jo and Clare just avoided her completely and kept out of the way.

It was the last week of the school term, and so there was no homework that night. Some said it was because the teachers didn't want to have to mark any papers – but no one grumbled too loudly! And Helen was glad, because it meant that she could dash home quickly and get ready for the barbecue. She climbed into a comfortable old pair of jeans and pulled a favourite green sweater on over the top of her school shirt – hoping her mother wouldn't notice and make her change into something else. She had arranged to meet Pat at her house, and then walk round to the next road where Dave and Ann lived. It was nice to be with friends again!

'Hallo, Pat – Helen – make yourselves at home.' Ann welcomed the two girls, and ushered them out through the back door into a tiny garden, already filled with people. The barbecue was burning well, and there was a delicious smell of sausages and burgers wafting into the air. Helen recognised many of the people she had seen on Sunday afternoon.

'Here you are, kids – help yourselves!' called Dave, placing a tray of hot dogs and burgers at the side of the barbecue. 'There's some ketchup and other revolting things on the little table over there,' pointing to a small folding table, which held all kinds of different relishes and sauces.

Helen and Pat joined in the general crush for food, and for the next ten minutes or so everyone was reasonably quiet, as they made short work of Dave's cooking, and were soon demanding seconds. Ann had made green salad and rice salad to go with the meat, and fruit salad or trifle to finish off with. You needed healthy appetites whenever you came to this house!

When everyone had eaten as much as they could manage – and some more than they could manage! – Dave and Ann helped themselves to coffee and joined the others. Dave flopped down beside Helen, and asked how she was getting on, and if she had enjoyed the evening.

'Yes, thanks,' said Helen. 'It's been really good. I think I've eaten more than I should though!'

Dave laughed and pointed to his own large expanse of stomach.

'You've got a way to go yet before you're a real size!' he said.

Helen wanted to ask him about God and reading the Bible, but she wasn't sure what to say. She wanted to tell him about the struggle she was having with Jo and Clare, but now he was here and she had an opportunity to speak, the words she had practised in her head wouldn't quite come out. She felt shy when it came to knowing how to start.

'You came with Pat, didn't you?' Dave said. 'Do you go to the same school?'

'No, we don't. Well, I mean, yes – er, we go to different schools, but we do go to the same riding school. That's where we met.'

'Oh, so you're another rider, then?' grinned Dave. 'I know Pat's been on about riding for ages, but Jeremy's much more sensible and has joined our football club!'

Helen grinned back at him.

'Football's all right, I suppose,' she said, 'especially if you're a boy. But I've always liked riding. I used to have a pony of my own.'

'Really? Bit expensive, aren't they?'

'We haven't got one now,' said Helen, sadly. 'So I suppose going to a riding school and riding someone else's ponies is the next best thing.'

They chatted on for several minutes about ponies and riding, and Dave told her that he'd never ridden in his life, but his wife Ann had – maybe she should talk to her. Helen felt a bit disappointed. She usually liked talking about riding to anyone, but she had really wanted to ask Dave about God and reading the Bible, and she thought it would be easy. But it wasn't. Why couldn't she just ask him what he thought about Jo and Clare? Or what to do when she felt God was wanting her to do something that was really too hard? Was it always difficult to do what God wanted?

Suddenly she paused and took a deep breath.

'Could I ask you a question?'

'Sure.' Dave was surprised at her sudden serious face.

'I'm trying to be a Christian – right?'

Dave nodded.

'Well, it's not easy, is it?'

Dave nodded again, and waited for her to continue.

Somehow Helen didn't know how to tell him about Jo and Clare. She didn't know how to say it without it sounding as if she were just tale-telling. And she wasn't sure that it was good to tell him how horrible someone else was, especially when he didn't know them, and had no real way of judging if what she said was right or fair.

'There are these two girls at school – and at the riding school,' she began. 'And they don't like me, and I've tried to be friends, but they don't want to be. And well . . . er . . . I don't really know what to do about it. And then you said that God will show us what to do if we ask him, and he can tell us what he wants us to do if we read the Bible. But, you see, when I read this bit in the Bible I wasn't sure . . . how do you know if it's God telling you to do something, or if it's just you imagining it, or what? And, anyway, how can you do it when it's too difficult?'

Helen screwed up her face and shrugged her shoulders. What a mess she'd made of it! The words had all come out wrong, and she hadn't said what she'd wanted to say at all. Now Dave would think she was stupid and didn't know what she was talking about.

'What did you read in the Bible?' he asked.

'Well, I didn't really know where to look. So I found this list of subjects, and it gave verses under each heading for you to look up. And I saw where it said about "what to do about enemies", and so I looked it up. But it didn't say how to beat enemies, like I thought it would.'

'What did it say?'

'It said you had to be nice to them. And pray for them. But I don't think I can do that. You don't know how awful they are!'

'It's not me who's asking you to do it – I'm not God!' smiled Dave. 'But do you think God is big enough to

55

change your situation if you do pray about it?'

Helen thought for a minute.

'I suppose so. But nothing seems to work. I have tried to be friendly, but they just won't be. Anyway, I thought if you were a Christian, God would be on your side and help you – not *them*. They don't care about anyone but themselves, and I don't suppose they care about God either,' she added.

'There's quite a lot there to think about, isn't there?' said Dave. 'Let's try to sort a few things out. First of all, I think you're right – God has spoken to you, and shown you what to do about these girls. It's not easy, but he will help you if you're willing to believe that he will, and do what he says. So I think we can pray for them – and for you – as a start.

'Then the next thing to remember is that God doesn't want you to get to the point that you hate them back when they hate you, because that will make you as bad as them. You can't be responsible for what *they* do and say – but you *are* responsible for what you do and say. So stop worrying about them for a minute, and try to be careful about how you behave. It's not easy when folk have a go at us, but God doesn't want us to kick them back. They'll find it difficult to fight when you don't fight back – the war has to stop at you. Do you see what I mean?'

'I think so.'

'Would you like me to pray about it with you now?'

Dave's question took Helen by surprise.

'What, here with all these people about?'

'Yes. Why not?'

Helen looked round. Everyone was busy chatting and no one seemed to be taking any notice of her or Dave.

'It'll be all right,' said Dave. 'No one will mind, or

even notice. After all, if we're Christians, what's wrong with just talking to God as much as we talk to each other? We often pray together here in ones or twos – you don't have to be in church to talk to him, you know.'

'OK.'

Dave leaned forward so that only he and Helen and Jesus would hear what he was saying. 'What are these girls called?'

'Jo and Clare.'

'Lord Jesus, thank you for showing Helen what you want her to do about Jo and Clare. You know how hard that is, because you had enemies too. Please help her not to hate them back, and please work things out so that they can make friends. Thank you that you care about Jo and Clare, and you love them even if they don't love you. Help Helen to care about them too. Thank you that you love Helen very much, and thank you that she's begun to believe in you and know you as her friend. Amen.'

'Amen.'

'Now,' said Dave, 'we need to help you a bit more with reading the Bible. It's not easy to read, is it?'

Helen grinned and shook her head.

'We use booklets in ETF called "One to One". They help you to read a bit of the Bible each day, and that way it's not too hard to cope with. I'll give you one to start you off, and see how you get on with it. We sometimes talk about reading the Bible in our Sunday afternoon meetings, because everyone finds it hard. But it does get better when we help each other. Want to give it a try?'

'Yes, please. And thanks for talking to me – and for the prayer,' added Helen, shyly. She was glad to talk to Dave, and felt that things would get better after all.

Chapter Eleven

Jo and Clare spent the remaining days of the school term avoiding Helen. But she didn't seem to mind. Even when they cut her dead, or turned and walked the other way whenever they saw her coming, it didn't seem to bother Helen.

By the time they all met on the first day of the pony holiday, Jo and Clare felt they were losing the battle. Helen seemed to be 'in' with everyone: Gail, Ted, Pat and some of the other girls as well. It was Jo and Clare who felt a bit out of things. And that made them feel even more miserable.

'Gather round, everybody,' Gail was saying. 'First job of the day is to catch the ponies in Long Field. I want you all to get a headcollar each – Helen, you pick up two – and wait for me in the back of the Land Rover.'

Everyone made a dash for the tack room and rummaged round to find the best headcollars.

'Here, you can have this one,' said Clare to Helen, throwing one over that was still covered in wet mud, and with a buckle that didn't work properly.

'*You* need two, though, don't you?' said Jo, unkindly. 'Try this one for size.' She tossed a tatty, broken head-collar across the tack room floor. The buckle caught Helen a nasty blow on her shin, and she had to rub her leg hard to cope with the hard sting. 'Oops, sorry,' smiled Jo, sarcastically. 'I should have aimed higher!' Jo and Clare giggled and went out of the tack room, carrying a headcollar each.

'Why're they being so nasty?' asked Sandra, one of the other girls.

'Search me,' said Helen, walking stiffly over to the Land Rover. 'Still, I don't care – they can please themselves.'

By the time Helen and the others reached the Land Rover and tried to climb in, Jo and Clare had spread themselves across the seats at the back. As Helen moved to sit down, one of them slid across to take up the space.

'So sorry!' they piped. 'We seem to have no room this morning . . .'

Things might have become worse, but Gail and Ted arrived at that moment. Gail climbed into the driving seat and Ted came round to the back to fasten the safety catches in place. 'Come on, you girls,' he said, 'everyone sit down properly. Stop messing about.'

They reached Long Field and the ponies were soon caught. As they led them back to the stables, Jo stroked Barney's neck. 'At least I've got you for the week, Barney,' she whispered. '*She's* not having you.' Somehow, though, things didn't feel right. Jo didn't usually fall out with people. But since Helen had come everything had gone wrong. She had spoiled just about everything. Gail and Ted liked Helen – even Barney had gone better for Helen than for *her*.

She looked at Barney as he walked quietly beside her. She didn't even feel the thrill and excitement any more that she had always had being with ponies. What was wrong? She had looked forward to this week for ages and now it had begun she felt fed up and miserable.

'OK, everyone – I want these ponies looking really shiny – you've got twenty minutes – there are some new brushes in the tack room – not enough for everyone, so please share them and take turns with the old and the new ones.' Gail's instructions were followed by a rush of girls to the tack room. No one minded *sharing* so long as it didn't have to be them!

Helen managed to get hold of a new dandy brush and body brush, although all the new curry combs and stable rubbers were grabbed by the others.

'I think *we're* meant to have these – we've been here longer than you,' said Clare, and she made a quick grab at the new brushes Helen was carrying.

'Get off!' said Helen, suddenly angry. She'd put up with being bullied for too long. As she elbowed her way past Clare she pushed her hard. Clare was taken by surprise and sat down with a bump. Pat laughed and ran out after Helen.

'I'll get you for this, you little worm,' hissed Clare. 'You wait!'

Jo helped her friend to her feet. This was war. There was no turning back now. Helen had asked for trouble, and she would get it!

60

Chapter Twelve

All the girls on the holiday were divided into two Rides – A and B. A was for the more experienced, and B for novice riders. Jo and Clare and Helen were all included in Ride A, of course, and Pat was in Ride B.

Barney went reasonably well that morning, though Jo still felt miserable every time she watched Helen riding her horse, Captain, with obviously more skill than either herself or Clare. And she hated it every time Gail said, 'Well done, Helen, that was good' – which she seemed to say all the time. Gail was puzzled why Jo and Clare were not their usual cheerful selves.

'What *is* the matter with you two this morning?' she asked. 'You're just not thinking about what you're doing, are you? I hope you're not going to be in this mood all week!'

'I'm not *in* a mood,' muttered Clare, under her breath. 'Just keep me out of the way of your precious little pet Helen, that's all . . .'

Why did she have to come and spoil everything? thought Jo. We were all right till *she* turned up! I don't think this week's going to be so good after all!

Jo and Clare went off by themselves at lunch time to eat their sandwiches, and make their battle plans.

'We've got to think of a way of making her look stupid,' Clare said, 'then maybe Gail and the others will stop saying she's so marvellous and good at everything.'

'Perhaps she'll fall off and break something – that would get rid of her – at least for a bit,' said Jo. 'Still, there's not much chance of that, is there? She's too blinking good!'

'She's going to spoil the whole week, you know.'

Both girls sat in silence. Neither of them could think of an idea to get at Helen. In the end, they gathered up their lunch boxes and empty lemonade cans, and made their way back to the tack room. As they arrived, Gail was pinning a list on the notice board.

'There you are, you two,' she said, with a welcoming smile – hoping to cheer them up. 'I've just put up the list of rides for this afternoon, but if you'd like to get your ponies ready – we have decided to have a change-over for the ride at 2.30. You can prepare the pony you "own" for this week, but ride the one you're down for on the list.'

'That's not fair,' grumbled Clare, 'I don't want to change.'

'Neither do I,' said Jo. 'Why do we have to do that?'

'Because,' Gail said, patiently, 'it's not good for you to ride the same pony all the time – this way you can widen your experience. Anyway,' she added, looking at Jo, 'you're on a horse this afternoon, rather than a pony, so that should be challenge enough for you!'

Gail moved away, and left all the girls scrambling round the notice, each one anxious to see who they would be riding.

Jo groaned when she read her name next to Captain.

'Just look what I've got!' she grumbled to Clare. 'That old gray nag should have been pensioned off years ago.

He's so slow and doddery, you can hardly call him a horse at all. PLUS the fact that he's Helen's for this week!'

'Look who's got your Barney,' said Clare, pointing to Helen's name. 'Trust her! Well, at least I've got Pippa, and she's quite nice.'

'Do you mean to say I've got to groom Barney so *she* can ride him?' Jo stormed out of the tack room and walked over to the stalls where the school ponies were tied, resting after their midday feed. Barney turned to look at her as she walked in. 'Barney,' she said, burying her face in his shaggy mane. 'I don't want her to ride you – do you think you could be really bad this afternoon? Give her a rotten ride . . .' She knew, of course, that Barney couldn't understand, but she felt better having told him how she felt. 'I've got to ride *her* rotten Captain,' she whispered, 'but I'll have you again tomorrow.'

2.30 arrived. Jo trailed over to collect Captain. He stood about 15.3 hands high, and she had never ridden anything so big. He had been a dark dappled gray once, but now he was snowy white with age, and his head seemed gaunt, stuck at the end of a long, skinny neck. His withers stood high and bony, leading down to long sloping shoulders. His eyes were big and kind, with great hollows above them, making them seem even bigger. Even though he was tall, he was gentle and stood quietly as Jo approached.

'Hallo, Captain,' said Jo, quietly, patting his neck. 'I don't really want to ride you – but I suppose you can't help being old and past it.' Captain stood perfectly still as Jo tightened his girth and tried to mount. She hadn't reckoned on how big he was. She lowered the stirrup two or three holes and tried again.

'Bit big for you, young lady,' chuckled a voice behind her. Jo glanced miserably over her shoulder to see who was speaking. Ted smiled his toothy grin as he watched her trying to mount.

'Hallo, Ted,' said Jo, 'just look what I've been given to ride! I can't even get on!'

'Here,' suggested Ted, 'I'll give you a leg up.' Ted held Jo's left leg, and with a quick '1–2–3', lifted her high above Captain's saddle. Jo felt as if she would never get down again! 'Your girth needs tightening,' said Ted, unceremoniously pushing her leg forward in front of the saddle flap. 'You should always check the girth *after* you get on as well as before, you know.'

'Why is that, Ted?' asked Jo. 'It was really quite tight before I got on.'

'That's because your horse blows his sides out against the girth, and sometimes it can be quite slack by the time he's breathed in again. Now mind you ride Captain well – he's been a grand horse in his day. You just need the slightest aid to tell him what you want.'

'Thanks, Ted,' said Jo, trying to raise a smile. But she didn't feel like it. She didn't want to be riding Captain, and – even worse – she didn't want Helen to be riding Barney.

All this time Captain had stood quite still. Now, as Jo gathered up her reins and sat up straight, it was as if he had switched himself on. Jo pressed down and in with the inside of her legs, and Captain moved forward with a long, swinging stride that quite took her by surprise. He moved rhythmically and she sensed a clear one-two-three-four as each hoof touched the soft peat floor of the school. She increased the feel on his mouth, and was thrilled as Captain responded by raising his head. Gail was standing in the centre of the school, watching.

'Increase the pressure slightly with your legs, Jo, just behind the girth.' Jo did. And Captain's hindquarters moved underneath him into a more collected position; his neck curved into a beautiful arch and the position of his head was almost vertical as he accepted the bit, and Jo began to feel as if she was moving in total harmony with him as he walked. She had never experienced the feel of a thoroughbred who responded almost to her thoughts, and it was wonderful. Once again she was totally absorbed in her world of horses.

Gail allowed the girls to walk round the school and settle down for a few minutes before positioning the various horses and ponies, with Captain as leading file. Jo squeezed his sides firmly and quietly with her legs – there was no need to use her heels at all, and Captain responded by moving in an even, extended walk to the front of the ride. He marched forward as if on parade, his head held high and interested in all that was happening. Jo found his trot a little difficult to get used to at first as Barney's steps were much shorter and quicker. But Captain moved evenly and she found him responding, as Ted had said, to the slightest aid from her hand or leg. When Gail asked her to go forward into canter, Jo sat low in the saddle, pressing down with her seat muscles and carefully squeezed with her inside leg on the girth and outside leg behind it. Captain seemed to come right underneath her, and suddenly she was cantering effortlessly and slowly along the side of the school. The feeling was so fantastic, it made Jo gasp with astonishment and pleasure. She had never experienced anything like this before on a horse, and she suddenly realised how wrong she had been about Captain. At the end of the ride, everyone dismounted, and Jo, flushed with pleasure, stroked Captain's face. 'You're fantastic!'

she told him, 'Sorry I was so wrong about you – you're not an old nag after all.' For a moment, Jo had forgotten all about Helen and Barney. As she looked up she saw Helen leading *her* pony out of the school. Perhaps you can be wrong about people, too, she thought, maybe Helen's not so bad after all. But then she saw Clare coming towards her, leading Pippa, and she pushed the thoughts about Helen out of her mind.

'Captain was great!' she said to Clare. 'Did you see that collected canter? It was almost like cantering on the spot!'

'It was OK. But I shall be glad to have my own pony again tomorrow. I've got a rotten headache. Come on, we're supposed to brush them off and turn them out in the field here today. If you don't hurry up The Lady Helen will be turning your Barney out.'

'She'd better not!' said Jo, 'she's only riding him today – he's still *my* pony for the week.'

But somehow her thoughts about Helen didn't seem quite so bad now. She had been wrong about Captain – and she had enjoyed riding him, she almost hoped she might ride him again before the week was out. But how could she do that if Captain was Helen's for the week?

Everyone returned to their own horse or pony to brush them over and turn into Home Field. This field was not as big as Long Field, but was more convenient when the school ponies were being used every day. Saddles and bridles were removed, and everyone scrubbed hard with dandy brushes to rub away the sweat marks from the ponies' backs and necks. Competition was high, and everyone wanted their pony to look the best.

'When you've brushed them over, bring them into Home Field,' instructed Gail. 'Don't forget to lead them right into the field and turn them round before letting them go. And don't forget to leave Pixie's headcollar on so we can catch him easily in the morning.'

'Why do we have to turn them round before letting them go?' Pat asked Helen.

'So that you are nearest to the gate, and if they decide to turn and gallop off, you won't get in the way – like that!' added Helen, as one of the girls slipped her pony's headcollar off, and he ducked his head and shot backwards before turning and thundering off, fully enjoying his freedom. Captain and Barney walked away more sedately, and found a patch of muddy ground. Captain stood and pawed the ground for a moment, then his knees buckled beneath him, and he rolled down on to the ground with a contented grunt. Barney followed suit, and soon they were both rolling over and over, enjoying the cool feel of sticky mud on their backs.

'I'm going to have to brush all that off in the morning!' sighed Helen. 'Just look at him!' For good measure, Captain lay on his side and rubbed his head delightedly in the mud. Then he and Barney stood up and shook themselves.

'At least, there's some dirt we won't need to brush off!' laughed Jo, as clouds of dust rose from the horse and the pony.

Helen turned and smiled at Jo. Jo half smiled back – but then she suddenly remembered they weren't supposed to be friends. She stepped back from the gate and walked over to the tack room to begin cleaning Barney's saddle and bridle. She began to wish she hadn't fallen out with Helen after all.

Chapter Thirteen

'I'm feeling really sick, Jo,' Clare said as the two of them made their way home that evening. Jo looked at her friend. She certainly looked pale and had dark rings round her eyes.

'Hope you're going to be all right,' said Jo, not knowing what else to say.

But Clare wasn't all right. She was ill for most of that night, and her mum said she wouldn't be able to go out at all the next day.

'Can't I see her?' said Jo.

'I don't think you should, dear,' said Clare's mother. 'You go off to the stables and we'll just have to hope she's feeling better by tomorrow. It might only be a chill she's caught, and a day in bed will soon put her right again.'

'She's *got* to be OK,' frowned Jo, 'we're getting ready for the gymkhana at the end of the week, and we were going to ride together in the partners' race.'

Jo hated leaving her friend, but it seemed she didn't have a choice. And without Clare at the riding school, she felt lonely – especially as Helen seemed to have made friends with everyone else.

Next afternoon, Clare felt much better and joined the

group, although she didn't feel well enough to ride. She stood in the indoor school with Gail watching the others. Gail had said they could practise a few races for the gymkhana to be held at the end of the Own a Pony Week, and as Clare was not needing her pony, Helen could ride him instead. It made sense to everyone, as, although Captain was great for riding in the school, he was a bit big for the scrambling on and off which would be needed in the races. Everyone thought that was a good idea. Everyone, that is, except Clare and Jo.

'Have you heard,' whispered Jo to Clare, when she had the opportunity, 'they've given your Nelson to Helen to ride?'

'Right!' said Clare, 'That's it. She's had it. I'm not having that.'

'But what can you do about it?'

'You'll see,' replied Clare, staring sullenly at Jo. 'I'll sort her out once and for all. I'm going to make sure she falls off – she's *not* riding Nelson!'

All the girls from Ride A collected in the middle of the school. The ponies had been working quite hard – as had the riders! – and everyone was glad of a breather before the races began.

'OK!' shouted Gail, 'everyone gather up at this end, and we'll try a straight relay race for starters.' Eight ponies and riders jostled together down one end of the school. Clare walked over to where Helen sat on Nelson. Helen drew back as she approached, not knowing what to expect.

'I think your girth could do with tightening a bit,' Clare said to Helen. 'Nelson does blow out a lot when you first get on. Here, would you like me to check it for you?'

Helen was surprised, but pleased at what seemed a

really friendly offer. 'Thanks,' she said, and lifted her leg forward in front of the saddle flap as Clare reached for the girth straps. But instead of tightening them, she quietly lowered them both down several holes, so that the girth was dangerously loose underneath Nelson's belly.

'That should do the trick,' smiled Clare, stepping backwards. All the girls in the first relay were in pairs. Helen was first to go in her pair. Each rider had to race to the far end of the school, sharply turn round a marker, collect a small cone that was balanced there, and gallop back, handing the cone to the second team member, whose job it was to race again to the marker, replace the cone and gallop back to their partner. The first two to complete the race were the winners. Even though it was only a trial run for the real gymkhana, excitement was high, and the ponies too could sense the fun and were livelier than usual. Everyone was raring to go!

'On your marks . . . get set . . . GO!' Four ponies shot forward almost before Gail had finished saying GO. They raced at full speed for the far end of the school, and turned on their haunches, as the riders used legs and hands frantically to bend them round the markers. Helen reached out to grab the cone, and as she did so her saddle slid round Nelson's sides and she was suddenly aware of the thunder of flailing hooves and wind that whistled past her ears as she fell sideways off the pony's back. For a split second it seemed as if her foot would be caught in the stirrup, and she would be dragged along the ground, but suddenly the stirrup iron broke free and she was flung hard against the side wall of the school. Nelson kicked at the uncomfortable saddle that was now swinging underneath him, and half cantered, half bucked his way back to the other ponies at the far end of the school.

For just a brief moment everyone stood quite still, staring in shock at what had happened. Then someone reached forward and grabbed hold of Nelson, and Gail ran over to where Helen lay, still and silent against the school wall. Helen opened her eyes, and tried to sit up then cried out with alarm as pain shot through her arm and across her whole body. 'Sit still a minute,' said Gail, 'don't try to move.' She could see the lower part of Helen's arm sticking out, making an ugly mis-shape underneath her sweater.

'I'm all right, I can get up,' said Helen, 'it's just my arm that hurts.'

I'm not surprised, thought Gail, it looks well and truly broken to me. Aloud she said, 'Take your time, Helen. Is it just your arm that's hurt, do you think? How does the rest of you feel?'

'OK,' whispered Helen. Then tears of pain and shock filled her eyes, and she groaned as Gail supported her. Carefully and slowly Gail and Ted (who had come hurrying into the school) helped Helen to her feet, and gently led her out.

'Jo,' said Gail over her shoulder, 'I'll leave you and Clare in charge for a moment. Everyone can take the ponies back into the yard and untack them, then get on with tack cleaning. Ted will be along in a few minutes to help with turning out.'

Jo and Clare looked at each other. No one spoke. Those who were still sitting on their ponies dismounted, and ran the irons up the stirrup leathers and led the ponies out of the school in a neat, silent line. All the feeling of fun and excitement had disappeared. Even the ponies were quiet and subdued. A few minutes later the girls were gathered in the tack room, miserably cleaning tack. Still no one said anything. Then suddenly the five girls from Ride B burst into the tack room.

'What's happened to Helen?' said Pat. 'Is it true there's been an accident? Where is she?'

'She fell off Nelson.'

'We don't know how badly she's hurt – Gail and Ted took her off to the office. I think they've sent for an ambulance.'

'No, they haven't,' said someone else. 'Gail drove Helen off in her car – I suppose she's taken her to the hospital.'

'Do you think she'll die?'

Jo and Clare, who had not spoken at all, looked at each other. 'You did something to make it happen, didn't you?' hissed Jo to Clare. 'What did you do?'

'Nothing,' whispered Clare, 'I didn't do anything. The saddle slipped, didn't it? It was nothing to do with me.'

Jo felt sick. She was sure that somehow Clare had caused the accident. Supposing Helen was badly hurt? Or even died? Why were things so awful? Surely Clare would own up if she had done something.

Clare felt sick, too. Sick with fear – Helen would be sure to say it was her fault. She would know that Clare had loosened the girths instead of tightening them. Supposing she did die? She'd only meant her to fall off and be made to look silly – she hadn't meant anything really bad like this to happen. Clare was scared.

Chapter Fourteen

Helen's mum looked pale and strained as she hurried down the hospital corridor. Gail was sitting beside Helen, who lay quite motionless on the hospital trolley in Casualty.

'Your daughter is here, Mrs Gray,' said the nurse. 'The doctor is just coming to see you.'

'Is she all right?' Helen's mother kept asking.

'Please don't worry,' said the nurse, 'she's in shock, but she'll be fine. She has been down to X-ray, and she has a broken arm – but the doctor will explain everything in just a minute.'

Gail rose to her feet and moved aside so that Helen's mother could sit down.

'Mrs Gray, I'm so dreadfully sorry. It was an awful accident – the saddle simply slipped round – I can't understand it. Helen is such a careful rider and all our pupils are taught the importance of tightening the ponies' girths.'

Mrs Gray tried to smile reassuringly at Gail, but she said nothing. She sat and laid her fingers gently across Helen's hand.

'Mrs Gray,' said a voice behind her, 'I'm Dr Martyn. Would you like to come into my office for a moment?'

Mrs Gray looked at her daughter and then at Gail.

She stood up and followed the doctor.

'Helen has an open compound fracture to her left arm,' explained Dr Martyn. 'We need your permission to give her an anaesthetic as this will be necessary so that we can set her arm in plaster.'

'She is going to be all right?'

'Oh, yes, nothing to worry about. She'll be uncomfortable for a while, but there's certainly no reason to think there'll be any complications. We'll keep her in hospital for a couple of days – but after that, I expect she'll quite enjoy the attention – most children like to see how many signatures they can collect on a plaster cast!'

Mrs Gray smiled a little shakily.

'Well, it's a relief to know things are no worse,' she said. 'I've been praying and trying to trust God for Helen's safety, but I have to admit I've been worried as well.'

'Who wouldn't be? Children are a precious gift and responsibility, aren't they? And utterly irreplaceable.'

Helen's mum smiled at him.

'Thank you,' she said.

Suddenly she knew that everything was going to be all right.

By the time Gail got back to the stables, the ponies had all been turned out, the tack cleaned, and the girls were all waiting anxiously to know what had happened. They crowded round as she got out of the car, although Jo and Clare stayed at the back.

'What happened?'

'Is she all right?'

'Has she broken her arm?'

'Now, please, just calm down everybody,' said Gail, waving them all into silence. 'Yes, Helen has broken her arm. But she's going to be all right. When I left, the doctor and her mother were with her, and they were explaining what was going to happen.'

'Did she cry?'

'She will be able to ride again, won't she?'

'Poor Helen. Did you see her? – the saddle slid right underneath . . .'

'It was horrible.'

'Is she going to have a plaster on?'

'I had a plaster on my arm once – it's all right to begin with, but it itches something awful at the end.'

Gail explained that Helen would have to wait a couple more hours before they could set her arm in plaster, as it wasn't safe to have an anaesthetic too soon after eating. Then she would have to stay in hospital for a couple of days – after that, it was just a case of waiting for six weeks or so until the break mended.

'And I hope it's a lesson to all of us,' Gail told them, 'that it's *very* important always to check your girths.' Everyone nodded. Clare stared down at her jodphur boots and poked the ground with her whip.

'Now, I think we've all had enough for one day,' Gail concluded. 'It's time you were on your way home – see you tomorrow.'

The crowd dispersed, and the girls moved away to collect their things. Suddenly, Gail turned as she remembered something.

'Oh – Jo and Clare – can you spare a minute?' she said.

The knot inside Jo's stomach tightened, and Clare suddenly felt sick and a bit weak at the knees. This was it – Helen had obviously told Gail about the way she had loosened Nelson's girth. Numbly, both girls slowly followed Gail as she walked across to the office.

75

Chapter Fifteen

Helen's mum and dad both came to see her the next morning. Dad wasn't able to stay too long, as he had to go to work, but Helen was glad that they were there.

'I'll have to go now, love,' he said, standing up. 'At least, you look a lot better than when I saw you last night.'

'Bye, Dad, see you later.'

He bent down and kissed his daughter, taking care not to lean on her left arm, now encased in its thick plaster cast. 'See you tonight – mind you behave yourself!'

'Fat chance to do anything else like this!' laughed Helen. She had slept fitfully all night, and her arm ached a lot, but now that morning had arrived, she felt better.

'They said I could get up soon – and come home tomorrow,' Helen told her mother. 'How long do you think it will be before I can ride again?'

'I'm not sure, dear. We'll have to see how quickly it mends. I think you'll just have to be patient.'

'Fancy missing the last day of the Own a Pony Week, though!' groaned Helen. 'I was really looking forward to the gymkhana. Now I shall miss it all. It's not fair.'

'I know. I'm sorry,' said her mum. 'Have you any idea what happened? Why was your girth so loose –

surely you know to tighten it *after* you get on as well as before?'

'Of course I do. I can't understand it – wait a minute! I do remember now! But surely she wouldn't . . .' Helen's voice trailed off in disbelief. 'Mum – you know what? Just before the race Clare came up and told me that Nelson's girth needed tightening, and she offered to do it for me. She must have loosened it instead – on purpose.'

Helen's mother frowned. 'Helen, are you sure? Why would she do such a thing?'

'Well, she's made it pretty obvious she doesn't like me – even more so than Jo. In fact, I almost think Jo and I could have been friends if it wasn't for Clare. But now we're all enemies.'

'But that's awful, Helen,' said her mum.

'I'm going to get even with her,' said Helen, bitterly. 'Of all the rotten, mean tricks . . . she *wanted* me to fall off, didn't she? She's always hated me. And I've never done anything to her – or to Jo. Well, she's not getting away with it this time – I'm fed up with her being so spiteful!'

For a moment Helen forgot about keeping her left arm still and she lifted the heavy plaster cast. Sharp pain shot from her fingers and through her arm and seemed to make her whole body gasp with shock and pain. Her eyes filled with sudden tears and she groaned as she gingerly lowered her arm back on the sheets.

'Mum, it does hurt,' she said, and the tears that had gathered in her eyes spilled over and ran down her cheeks, making tiny wet splashes on the bed cover.

'I know, love,' said her mum. 'But the worst *is* over and it will get better. You've just got to be patient and give it time. It could've been much worse, couldn't it?

At least you've only got *one* broken arm and the rest of you is OK. Thank God,' she added in a tiny voice.

'God?' repeated Helen. The tears had stopped now and she stared angrily at her mother. 'I thought he was supposed to be my friend. Didn't protect me from Clare's horribleness, did he? It seems being a Christian doesn't really help at all – things have got worse, not better!'

'How can you say that?' said Helen's mum, gently. 'You had an accident – caused by someone else – and you broke your arm. But you could have broken both arms, or both legs, or your neck, or back – or been killed! Helen – we have a *lot* to say "thank you" to God for – and don't let's forget it!'

They were both silent for a moment, struggling to take in what had happened.

'I'm tired, Mum,' said Helen at last. 'I don't really like being enemies with Clare or Jo or anybody. Why do people have to be like that? There was no reason why we had to fall out, was there? I just know I want it to end now – I'm fed up with the struggle.'

'Would you like me to talk to Jo and Clare?'

There was another pause. Then Helen said, 'No, I don't think so. It won't do any good.'

'Maybe we should talk to Gail at the riding school?'

Helen pulled a face. She didn't really want a big scene with Gail, or Jo and Clare. She just wanted to be friends and enjoy riding again.

'Do you really think that God can do anything about it?' she said at last.

'I'm quite sure he can,' said her mum. 'I don't expect he likes the situation any more than we do.'

'What do you think a Christian should do, then, about people who won't be friends, and only want to be enemies?'

Helen's question took her mother by surprise – she was busy trying to come to terms with her own feelings, and was not quite ready to cope with such a direct challenge!

Mrs Gray swallowed hard and thought for a moment. 'Well,' she said at last, 'you have to ask yourself "What would Jesus do?" '

'And?'

'Jesus loved his enemies, didn't he? And he prayed for them. He wants us to do the same. That's the only way enemies can change into friends.'

Helen looked down at her plastered left arm. The tips of her fingers were just visible curling out of the end.

'But that's really hard. How can I pray for Jo and Clare? You must be kidding. Look what they did to me!'

'Sure, it's not easy,' said her mum, 'but Jesus didn't find it easy, either. Look what his enemies did to him.'

'You mean the cross and all that?'

'That's right. Even as they nailed him to the cross, Jesus asked God to forgive them. So he knows just how hard it is to "love your enemies and pray for them", because he did it himself. You have to decide whether you want to deal with things in *his* way, or go on being enemies.'

Helen's eyes filled again with tears. Her mum's did, too, though she quickly made sure that Helen didn't see them. Although she didn't want to admit it to Helen, she was really quite worried that things were going from bad to worse, and she was shocked to think that Clare had deliberately caused the accident. She wasn't too sure how to deal with the situation – and she knew that she, too, needed God's help and guidance just as much as Helen did. Perhaps she should go and talk to Gail about what had happened.

'Look, Helen,' she said at last, 'why don't we ask Jesus to help us now? We could pray that he will show you how to make friends with Jo and Clare, and stop all this silly enemy business before it gets any worse.'

Helen nodded. Then together they asked Jesus to help them and to put an end to the 'enemy' situation with Jo and Clare.

Chapter Sixteen

Gail rummaged through the pile of papers on the desk, and opened and closed the desk drawers in quick succession.

'How is it,' she muttered, 'that you can never find something when you want it!'

Jo and Clare stood, silent and waiting, hardly daring to think what Gail wanted to say to them.

'Here it is!' said Gail, triumphantly pouncing on the small cash box she had been looking for. She opened it, took out a five pound note, and handed it to Clare. Both girls stared at Gail, mystified. This was certainly not what they had expected!

'Right!' said Gail. 'I'm going to ask you two for a favour. I have to stay behind here and clear up at the stables, and by the time I leave all the shops will be shut. I wondered if you could call at the gift shop on your way home – you know, the nice one at the bottom of Foley Hill – and buy a card and gift of some kind that we can all send to Helen? I thought you would be the best people to choose something, as you know her well, don't you? You all go to the same school?'

Jo and Clare didn't dare look at each other. Jo stared at the floor, and Clare at the five pound note.

'Well? Will that be OK?' said Gail.

'Yes, sure,' muttered Clare.

'Sure,' echoed Jo.

'That's all right then,' Gail said, locking up the cash box and returning it to a drawer, so it could be lost and looked for again when it was next needed! 'Poor Helen,' she continued, 'She's going to miss the gymkhana tomorrow, and she was doing so well. Still, we have to be grateful it was nothing worse than a broken arm, don't we?'

'Yes,' whispered Jo.

'Mm,' said Clare.

'Look – is everything all right with you two?' Gail was puzzled by their attitude, but she was also aware that she had a lot of work to do before she could leave that evening. 'If there's something bothering you, you only have to say.'

'No – everything's fine,' said Clare.

'Well, off you go, then, otherwise the shop will be closed if you leave it any later,' said Gail. And together the two friends turned and walked out of the office, leaving Gail still puzzling over them. She couldn't think what was the matter with those two – they used to be such good fun to teach, and now all their enjoyment seemed to have disappeared. But her thoughts didn't last too long, and soon she was busy helping Ted to finish off the stabled horses for the night, and making sure that all the school ponies were safe and secure in the field.

Jo and Clare collected their things, mounted their bikes, and slowly left the stable yard.

'What are we going to do?' said Jo.

Clare shook her head. 'I didn't really mean her to have an accident – well, not a proper one,' she added. 'Gail doesn't know, does she? She doesn't know what I did?' Jo had been really shocked when Clare had confessed to her secretly what she had done. But she felt she had to stand by her friend, no matter what.

'It doesn't seem like it,' answered Jo. 'But I think I'm as much to blame as you. We did rather gang up on her, didn't we?'

'Do you still hate her?'

'Helen? No, I just feel awful about what's happened. I wish we could turn things back and do things differently.'

'Do you think Helen's told her mother?'

'Don't know. Maybe we should call at her house and ask if we can go and see Helen tomorrow after the gymkhana. Gail might want us to deliver the present for everyone else – it might be easier if we had a present to take.'

'But what if she's told her mum?'

'Well, I expect it'll all come out sooner or later. We'll just have to say we're sorry.'

'I'm not sure I dare go to the house.'

'Well, have you got a better idea?'

The girls went into the gift shop and spent ages choosing a card, and even longer trying to select a gift. In the end they chose a china mug with ponies handpainted on it. The very effort of choosing a gift actually helped to cheer them up.

'You know, I'd quite like this for myself!' said Jo.

'I would, too,' said Clare. 'They say it's always easier to choose a present for someone else if you would enjoy it yourself! I think Helen will really like this.' For the first time they both began to feel friendly towards Helen. They were genuinely sorry about the accident. If only it hadn't happened! If only they could do something to put

83

things right!

Helen's mother was surprised when she answered the door, and saw Jo and Clare standing there. Her first and immediate reaction was to be angry, and then she remembered the prayer she and Helen had prayed earlier.

'Hallo – it's Jo and Clare, isn't it?'

'Yes.' Jo's voice seemed to come from a long way away. 'Yes,' she said again, trying to calm the tremble she felt as she spoke. 'We wondered if we . . . that is . . . we wondered how Helen is . . .'

'And whether it would be all right if we called to see her at the hospital tomorrow after the gymkhana,' finished Clare.

'Would you like to come in for a drink?' asked Helen's mum. 'You can leave your bikes here – they'll be quite safe. And you look as if you could do with a drink to cool you off.'

'Thank you.'

Jo and Clare followed Mrs Gray into the kitchen and perched themselves on the kitchen stools. No one spoke as Helen's mum poured two refreshing cold drinks for them, adding ice chunks from the freezer.

'There you go. Help yourself to a biscuit,' she added, pushing a tin towards them.

'Mrs Gray, we're really sorry about Helen's accident,' said Jo, ignoring the biscuits. 'We really are.'

'Yes, we are,' said Clare. She could hear her heart pounding, almost as if it were in her mouth. 'It started off as a bit of fun, really, but . . . er . . . I think it was because I . . . I did it,' she ended miserably. 'I loosened Nelson's girth, and that's why Helen fell off. I'm really very sorry.'

'We do want to be friends with Helen – if she's willing

to be,' said Jo. 'She's a much better rider than either of us.' Somehow Jo knew that was entirely irrelevant, but she was running out of words to say. She took a slurp of the cold drink, and sat staring into the glass, as if some kind of way out would suddenly appear there. This was definitely the worst moment in her life.

Helen's mother looked at them both. Suddenly she smiled, the friendliest of smiles. She put one arm round Jo and the other round Clare, and hugged them both. 'Thank you for being brave enough to say all that,' she said. 'I know that Helen will be only too thrilled to know that you want to be friends – that's what she's wanted all along. In fact, you may not realise it, but Helen has felt really desperate about the situation, and we didn't know what to do. We prayed to Jesus and asked him to help sort it out – and it looks to me as if he's done just that!'

Jo and Clare looked at each other in surprise.

'I don't really know anything about God,' said Clare. 'I never pray or anything like that.'

'You can know him, if you want to,' said Helen's mother. 'But you have to begin by turning away from the wrong things in your life, and asking his forgiveness. You have to ask Jesus to be in charge of your life, to be with you as your friend and guide for always.'

'I'd like that,' said Clare.

'So would I,' said Jo.

'Can we do it now?'

'If you want to. Would you like me to pray with you?'

Jo and Clare nodded. They were not used to praying like this. The only 'religion' they had experienced was at school, which meant very little to them, as they had not been interested and not bothered to listen. But this was different. They had never met anyone before who

85

actually seemed to know Jesus as a real person who would be your friend.

'Lord Jesus,' said Helen's mum, 'please help Jo and Clare to get to know you. They want you to be their friend – please show them how. Amen. OK, Clare and Jo, now Jesus is listening, so just tell him what you want to say.'

'Jesus,' began Clare, a little hesitantly, 'er, I mean, Lord Jesus, I'm not really sure how to do this, but I would like you to be my friend. I'm sorry for the things I've done wrong – especially about Helen and her accident. Amen.'

'Jesus,' said Jo, 'I want to know you, too. Please forgive me for the things I've done wrong – and please be my friend. Amen.'

'Amen,' said Helen's mum. 'That's it – you've asked him to be with you, to forgive you and be your friend, and now he will always be there.'

'How do you know?' said Clare. 'I don't feel any different.'

'Neither do I,' said Jo. 'It just seems strange talking to him, though, doesn't it? How can you know that you really are forgiven?'

'What a lot of questions you do ask!' laughed Helen's mum. 'He can forgive us because he died on the cross to pay for our forgiveness – it's free to us, but it cost Jesus his life! But that just shows how much he loves us, because he was willing to go through all that. Then, you have to work at a friendship, don't you? You can't expect to know everything all at once. It takes time. But there are certain things you can always be sure about. You can always be sure that Jesus loves you and wants the best for you; you can always be sure he will guide you and help whenever you ask him. Not that he's a kind of Father Christmas, as I'm always saying to Helen! Maybe the best thing to help you two would be to give you a booklet which explains a bit more about being a Christian. But one way of learning about Jesus is to join a good church.'

'But church is so boring.'

'I know some of them are – but if you go to one which is lively and friendly, and where they really know Jesus as a friend and Saviour, you'll learn a lot.'

Jo and Clare finished their drinks and a biscuit each. They both felt more like eating now.

'I feel much better,' said Jo.

'So do I,' said Clare.

'We all feel better when we've put something right that's been wrong, and been forgiven,' said Helen's mum. 'Now, look, I have to go down to the hospital to see Helen, and I'm sure you must be expected home. Helen will be home herself tomorrow afternoon. Why don't you ask your parents if you can come to tea and tell Helen all about the gymkhana. I know she's sorry to be missing it, but she'll be really pleased to see you both and hear how the Own a Pony Week ended.'

Both girls winced when they realised how disappointed Helen would be.

'But supposing . . .' Clare's voice trailed off.

'Supposing Helen doesn't want to be friends?' Jo finished off what they were both thinking. 'I wouldn't really blame her if she didn't.'

'That's for Helen to decide,' said Mrs Gray, 'but I'm sure she'll be so glad about it, you'll have no problems. Don't forget, she's already prayed about it – and Jesus has given his answer, so I'm sure everything will be fine. We've all learned a lot from what's happened. Don't worry about it any more – we'll see you both tomorrow for tea?'

'Yes – thank you very much.'

'And thank you for the drinks. And for the chat.'

Jo and Clare gathered up their things and went outside to collect their bikes.

'Thank you, Mrs Gray,' said Jo again, 'please give my love to Helen.'

'And mine,' added Clare.

Helen's mum smiled as she waved them off. 'Thank you, Lord Jesus,' she said, 'thank you so much!'

Chapter Seventeen

The day of the gymkhana had arrived, and all the girls were busy making sure that *their* pony was the cleanest and smartest. Coats were brushed till they shone. As it was a nice warm day, Gail said that manes as well as tails could be washed.

'Make sure you rinse them properly,' she said. 'You may like to plait your pony's mane and tail, so if you want to know how to do that, let me know, and I'll show you.'

Some of the Mountain and Moorland ponies' manes were not really meant for plaiting, and there were generally more sprouting ends than neat plaits, but everyone was praised for effort! Gail showed them how to take the tiny hairs at the base of the tail and gradually work down in a more or less straight plait to a few inches below the dock, and then turn the plait under and fasten off in a neat line down the centre of the tail.

The finishing touches were added to the grooming by painting neatsfoot oil round each hoof, and giving a final polish to the ponies' coats with a stable rubber. Marks were given for the best groomed pony and Ted, who was judge, had a hard job deciding. In the end he gave the prize to Jo with Barney from Ride A, and Sandra with Nettle from Ride B.

Then it was time for the gymkhana.

'I think I've used too much saddle soap on my saddle,' said Jo. 'Look how slippery it is!'

'My reins are, too,' said Clare. 'Still, they are clean and shiny.'

All the girls from both Rides were together for the games. The first race was a Walk-Trot-Canter relay race for teams of three; Gail was careful to ask the novice riders to ride at walk or trot, and those from Ride A to take canter. It was a good warm-up, and everyone enjoyed it. Next followed a sack race, then apple bobbing, when most of the ponies shied away from the water tubs – except Barney who decided to drink a mouthful of the water and make a grab at the apple before Jo had even dismounted!

The games continued, and Gail made sure that everyone won a rosette of some sort. At the end, sweaty ponies and riders trotted or cantered in a Victory Ride round the school, each proudly displaying at least one rosette. It had been the perfect end to a super holiday!

Ponies were untacked and lovingly brushed off for the last time. Manes and tails were unplaited, where they hadn't already come undone!

'Thank you, Barney,' said Jo, draping her arm round his neck. She rubbed the back of his ears and he lowered his head, enjoying the attention.

'Captain was nice to ride, but you're still the best,' she told him. Just then he smelled the Polos in the pocket of her jodhpurs, and butted her with his nose. 'OK, OK,' she laughed, 'you soppy thing – I get the message. I've saved the last two just for you.' Barney raised his head and watched as she undid the mints. His ears were pricked and so pointed they almost met over the top of his head. And he grunted at her to hurry up.

If food was being offered, he was for it!

'Gather round everyone,' Gail's call broke in on Jo's private conversation with Barney. All twelve girls emerged from various stalls and loose boxes and went to where Gail stood leaning on the tack room door. When they were all assembled, Gail produced the card and mug which Jo and Clare had bought the day before.

'We thought you'd all like to share in sending this gift to Helen,' she said, holding the china mug for everyone to see. 'And please all sign the card. Jo and Clare are taking the present to Helen on the way home this evening – so please make sure you add your name to the card before going home. Now you've all seen it, I'll wrap up our present. You two can collect it from the office as you go. OK?'

Jo and Clare nodded.

'Well,' continued Gail, 'that's it! Ted and I hope you've all enjoyed the week – it's been good to see how you've all improved in your riding and I hope you'll all continue to do that. One day we may see some of you show jumping or eventing – you never know! Now, if you'd like to collect your ponies, we'll turn them all out together – for the last time!'

'It's been a super week, Gail,' said Sandra, 'thanks for giving us such a good time.'

'Yes, thanks,' echoed the others.

Pat said 'thank you', then turned away quickly. She hated goodbyes, especially after enjoying such a wonderful week. She could feel tears pricking the back of her eyes, and she certainly didn't want anyone else to see! But she wasn't the only one!

'You know something, Ted?' said Gail, as the girls all moved away to collect their ponies, 'you can tell they've enjoyed themselves when they all say goodbye in tears!'

Ted grinned at her.

'I know,' he said. 'I shall never understand women!' But he smiled kindly as he picked up two feed buckets and walked across the yard to return them to the feed barn. It had been a good week – except for Helen, of course. But he knew she would enjoy the gift, and all the messages everyone had scribbled on the card. Nice girl, he thought to himself, best rider we've had here for ages – she'll be really good one day.

By the time Jo and Clare arrived at Helen's house, they were both feeling a little nervous. Supposing she didn't want to be friends with them? Supposing she hated them? Neither of them voiced their fears out loud, but they each knew how the other felt. Jo held the card and Clare the china mug. They also had their rosettes to show her.

'Here goes,' said Jo, as she reached out to ring the bell.

'Here goes,' echoed Clare in something less than a whisper.

Helen's mother opened the door, smiled warmly, and waved them in.

'Great! You made it in good time – do come in. Helen's in the sitting room – in there. You go and talk while I finish getting the tea.' Jo and Clare found themselves pushed into the room, where Helen sat reading a comic. The three girls stared rather solemnly at each other for a moment, then all broke the silence together.

'Hallo,' began Helen.

'We brought you . . .' said Clare.

'How are you . . . ?' said Jo.

Then they all laughed nervously. 'Well, that wasn't

such a good start, was it?' smiled Helen. 'I am really glad you came – Mum told me what you said, and I'm sorry, too, for the way I was feeling about you. But we can all be friends from now on, can't we?'

'Sure,' said Jo.

'I'd be really glad to be friends,' said Clare. 'I'm sorry for what happened.'

'Same here,' said Jo. 'How does it feel?' she added, pointing to Helen's left arm.

'It just aches a lot, but I suppose it will gradually get better. I think it has to be like this for about six weeks. Still – I'm hoping I'll be allowed to ride before then – my friend rode her pony when she had her arm in plaster, so I don't see why I shouldn't.'

There was silence for a moment, then Helen said: 'Tell me about the gymkhana, then. What happened? Was it good fun? Who won? How did Pat get on? I hope she managed to win something!'

'Yes, she did,' said Jo, 'in fact, we all won at least one rosette. Here's the one I won for Barney – for the Best Turned Out Pony – even though I didn't win any races!' Jo proudly showed Helen her rosette, and Helen held it in her right hand. 'It's lovely,' she said, 'it's really lovely.'

'You can keep it, if you like,' said Jo, quickly. She hadn't meant to give it away at all. She had even worked out where she could hang it in her bedroom – this was the first rosette she had ever won in her life, and she knew how proud her mum would be to see it and hear all about how she had won it. But then she suddenly realised how much Helen would like to have one. And she knew it was right to give it away instead of keeping it for herself.

'Can I? Can I really keep it?' said Helen, stroking the

bright silks on the rosette.

'Yes – do have it,' said Jo, generously. It was costing her a lot to give it up, but even as she did so, she was glad to bring pleasure to someone who previously she had hated and tried to hurt. 'Do have it,' she repeated, more for her own benefit, to let herself know she really meant it! 'I know if you'd been there today, you would have won more than just one rosette!'

'We brought this gift and card from us all,' said Clare, laying the package on Helen's lap. 'Hope you like it. We all signed the card – and everyone sent their love to you.'

'Oh thanks,' said Helen, 'er . . . do you think you could unwrap it for me? I'm not very good with one hand yet!'

The next minutes passed happily, as all the three girls talked non-stop about the gymkhana, and about which they thought were the best ponies at the riding school and which they were hoping to ride next. Helen admired the mug, and laughed at the different messages that the others had written for her on the card.

'Time for tea!' interrupted Helen's mum. 'Would you two like to go upstairs and have a wash and freshen up first? I don't mind stable-talk at meal times, so long as it's clean!'

Jo and Clare stood up. The three girls smiled at each other.

'I'm glad we're going to be friends from now on,' Jo said.

'So am I – we'll try not to make such a mess of things again, Helen,' said Clare. 'I think asking Jesus to help us will make it easier.'

'I never knew you could get to know God by having Jesus as a friend,' said Jo.

'Neither did I until a little while ago,' said Helen.

'But I'm going to learn all I can about being a Christian from now on.'

'Maybe we could come to your church with you and your mum, Helen?' said Jo.

'What a good idea. By the way,' said Helen, 'would you two like to be the first to sign my plaster? And, Jo, thanks for giving me your rosette – that's the very best gift of all!'